PIPER

JACQUELINE HALSEY

Nimbus Publishing Limited
3660 Strawberry Hill Street
Halifax, NS, B3K 5A9
(902) 455-4286 nimbus.ca

For my daughter Karen,
who can never resist an adventure.

Printed and bound in Canada
Design: Grace Laemmler Design
Cover and interior illustratons: James Bentley

NB1286

This story is a work of fiction. Names, characters, incidents, and places, including organizations and institutions, either are the product of the author's imagination or are used fictitiously.

Library and Archives Canada Cataloguing in Publication

Halsey, Jacqueline, 1948-, author
    Piper / Jacqueline Halsey.
    Issued in print and electronic formats.
    ISBN 978-1-77108-605-9 (softcover).--ISBN 978-1-77108-606-6 (HTML)
    I. Title.
PS8615.A3938P57 2018   C813'.6   C2017-907959-X
                                              C2017-907960-3

Nimbus Publishing acknowledges the financial support for its publishing activities from the Government of Canada, the Canada Council for the Arts, and from the Province of Nova Scotia. We are pleased to work in partnership with the Province of Nova Scotia to develop and promote our creative industries for the benefit of all Nova Scotians.

AUTHOR'S NOTE

Piper is a work of fiction. Some of the names in this story may be found on the *Hector*'s passenger list but the characters' stories and personalities are totally made up. Through the eyes of a twelve-year-old boy, I tried to imagine the voyage. I focused on the experiences and emotions of a family of settlers who, like many immigrants today, risked a dangerous journey to escape the repression of their homeland in hopes of a better life in a strange new country.

For more information on the Battle of Culloden, see The Story of the *Hector*, beginning on page 166, and for help with some of the Scottish Gaelic and nautical terms, visit the Glossary, beginning on page 169.

CHAPTER 1

"WE'RE DONE, DA," SHOUTED DOUGAL, AS HE and his friend Ruari heaved the last slab of peat into place.

"Done indeed," said Da, tousling Dougal's hair.

Dougal slapped the dirt off his hands and looked down the long wall of peat bricks drying in the wind. It stretched over the hill and way out of sight.

"This should keep our fires burning for a while," said Da, with a satisfied smile.

The villagers had been working together cutting the peat they used for fuel from the black bogs on the heath. The hard, dirty work had been going on for weeks, but it had been fun too, and getting dirty didn't bother Dougal. He was so busy admiring the peat wall and flapping away the annoying flies buzzing round his head that he didn't notice Ruari creeping up behind him.

"Found some more peat for you," said Ruari, showering a handful of the sticky black earth over Dougal's head.

"I'll get you back for that," shrieked Dougal chasing his friend, with a handful of peat destined for the back of his neck.

"Stop!" shouted Da. "If you lads have got that much energy, I'd better find you some more work."

"No, no," said Dougal. "We're really tired, aren't we Ruari?"

"Exhausted," said Ruari, and flopped down on a patch of springy heather to prove it.

"Behave yourselves," said Da, trying not to smile. He walked off to talk to the men.

Dougal sat down next to Ruari. The heather was green now, but by the end of summer it would turn the hills every shade of purple. That was Dougal's favourite time of year. He loved bringing in the harvest of oats and barley. Mam's garden would be bursting with turnips and beans. There'd be fish in the loch and plenty of berries to stuff in his mouth whenever he saw them. Just thinking about all that food made his empty belly growl.

Ruari gave him a shove. "You sound hungrier than me, but that's impossible."

"Don't know why our food never quite lasts 'til the next crop has grown," said Dougal with a huge sigh. "Mam's porridge is getting awfully thin these days."

"My da says we need more farmland," said Ruari, "but that costs money, and we haven't got any."

"Well the grass is beginning to grow, so at least our poor bony cows will have something to nibble on."

~~

Mam appeared over the hill with Wee Mary, Dougal's brand new baby sister, strapped snugly to her chest. His other sisters were with her too. Flora danced ahead while

Maggie, with Dolly tucked under her arm, clung tightly to Mam's skirt.

"You're a welcome sight," said Da, waving to his family. The men were taking a well-earned break in the late afternoon sunshine. They lit their pipes while Mam went round and filled their mugs with heather ale.

Da took a long drink then looked over at Dougal and Ruari. "Away wi' you boys. Go find something for your Mam's cookpots."

Dougal and Ruari let out a loud whoop.

"Be back in time for chores," added Ruari's father.

"We will," they chorused.

"And clean yourselves up," called Mam. "Your faces are so grimy, I can hardly tell you two apart."

Ruari raced off, but Dougal stopped to grab the basket he'd brought their lunch in. He'd need it for all the mussels he hoped to find. Flora got to it first. "I'll come with you," she said. "I know where there's wild thyme and dandelion greens."

"No. You can't come. Tell her, Mam." Dougal shot a desperate look at his mother. No way was he taking annoying Flora with him. His free time was far too precious.

"Give Dougal the basket, Flora," said Mam sternly. Her voice softened. "I'm going to show you where to find an herb you've never ever seen before. It grows in a secret place. Wait 'til I tell you what it can do."

Flora stuck her tongue out at Dougal and threw down the basket. He picked it up and chased after Ruari.

With the basket bumping against his leg, Dougal ran across the narrow strips of farmland. Getting the stony soil ready for planting would be tomorrow's work, but for now he was free to run with the wind. Even though

Ruari was a long way ahead, Dougal couldn't resist climbing over the large jagged rocks that poked through the heather. He loved climbing.

Mam had shown him a drawing of a tree in her herbal book. It had an enormous trunk with great branches that filled the sky. He'd often wondered what it would be like to climb that tree right to the top and find out what the sky felt like. Only scrubby little trees grew around his village in the windswept highlands of Scotland. They'd probably break if you tried to climb them.

Splashing through a last boggy section of heath, Dougal arrived at the seashore and caught up with Ruari. They stood and looked down at the other village kids already scrabbling around for shellfish in the rocky pools along the shore.

"There's not going to be much left for us," said Ruari. "We're not the only ones with noisy bellies."

"We'll have to go deeper then," said Dougal, stomping straight into the cold water. "Come on, the tide's going out, we might be able to get to the end of the headland, there's always mussels there."

The waves squeezed between the rocks, frothed to the shore, dragged themselves back, swelled and rushed in again. One minute the water was just above his ankles, the next it was up to his waist. It was a wild rocky coast and Dougal loved it.

He looked behind him to see how Ruari was doing. Big mistake—as he twisted round, a rogue wave snuck in sideways and caught him off balance. He sat down hard. The wave streamed over him, pulling him with it, then letting him go.

Ruari burst out laughing. "Need a rest already, Dougie?"

Dougal spat out a mouthful of ocean and wiped away the water dripping into his eyes. "Not funny."

Still laughing, Ruari held out his hand and pulled Dougal up. They staggered back to dry ground and sat on the shore. "It's too windy to go any further today," said Ruari. "Look at all the whitecaps on the ocean."

"Shame," said Dougal, taking off his vest and shirt. "A feed of shellfish would make a really good supper." He wrung as much water as he could from his clothes and laid them on the pebbles to dry off.

"Do you think that's a ship out there?" asked Ruari, pointing to the horizon.

Dougal squinted at the distant speck. "It's moving, so it must be a ship of some sort, but it's too far away to make out the masts or anything. Wonder where it's going?"

"It's following the sun," said Ruari, jumping up. "Which is going down fast. If I don't get home and see to our cows, I'll be in trouble. Let's try and catch the low tide tomorrow."

"I'm going to stay a bit longer," said Dougal.

"Suit yourself," said Ruari. He gave Dougal a wave and headed off towards his home.

The other children were leaving too, and soon Dougal was the only one left on the beach. He was beginning to shiver, but he didn't want to go home empty-handed. It was too cold to go back in the water but a search along the shoreline might turn up something edible the others had missed.

Dougal put his damp shirt back on and was about to pull on his vest when, out of the corner of his eye, he saw something move. He stood stock-still and very slightly turned his head. A rabbit was nibbling on a new clump of grass just a few feet away. Slowly and silently Dougal squatted down. He took his slingshot out of his pocket, picked up a pebble, carefully aimed, then let the shot go.

The rabbit dropped to the ground. It wasn't a very fat rabbit, but Mam would make it into a delicious stew with herbs and thick gravy. Dougal could almost smell it, and just the thought made his mouth water and his insides growl.

He picked up the rabbit. "Thank you, rabbit," he said. "I only shot you because we are all really hungry at home and we haven't had meat in a very long time."

Dusk was falling and the shadows were long and deep but Dougal knew the way home like the back of his hand. He jogged along, jumping over the familiar obstacles on the rough ground. A big grin spread over his face as he imagined Da and Mam's expressions when they saw what he'd caught. Maybe they'd ask Ruari to come over for dinner tomorrow.

He reached the well-worn path leading to his village. Down in the glen, edging a small clearing, lay a scattering of low stone cottages. Their shaggy, thatched roofs nearly touched the ground. They always reminded Dougal of a flock of ragged sheep ready to be sheared. Like the other cottages, his had no windows and the insides were black from the peat fire that burned day and night in the centre of the house. Mam's fire always made the dark house seem cozy, especially when something good—like rabbit stew—was simmering in her big cookpot.

Dougal stopped outside his home and tried his best to look serious, in order to tease Mam and Da before presenting them with his surprise. It was no good, he was too excited. He crashed through the door.

"Guess what I've got?" he yelled, hiding the rabbit behind him.

"You're soaked," said Mam. "What have you been doing and where's my basket?"

"Oh! I forgot it, but I caught a rabbit. Look, Da." He held the rabbit up by its back legs. "You said get something for Mam's cookpot. Rabbit stew tomorrow, eh?"

Mam took the rabbit from him, but she didn't seem very excited about it. Da didn't even turn round to look. He was sitting with his elbows on the table and his head in his hands. A deep scowl knitted his eyebrows together. "You're late and I've had to do half your chores," he growled.

"I was going to do them after supper," said Dougal. He looked up at Mam. "What's happened?"

"What's happened?" Da's voice thundered around the stone walls of the croft. He thumped the table, making the wooden bowls bounce. Flora sat very still and Maggie ran and hid Dolly behind Mam's skirt.

"The rent's gone up again. That's what's happened," said Da. "If we can't pay in money or grain we'll have to pay in animals."

"You mean they'll take our cows and our hens?" asked Dougal. "They can't do that."

"Seems they can," said Mam, putting a hand on his shoulder. "We barely made it through last winter. How we'll make it through the next, I don't know."

CHAPTER 2

"YOUR DA'S LATE TONIGHT," SAID MAM AS SHE ladled out the barley soup. "Wonder what's keeping him."

Since the news of the rent increase a few weeks ago, her eyes had taken on a worried look and her smiles seemed like pretend ones. Da was just plain angry. He stomped everywhere with his hands clenched in tight fists. Dougal had to admit, these days, he kind of liked the evenings when Da was late home.

He'd just dunked a chunk of bannock into his soup when the sound of Da's heavy footsteps thudded to a halt outside. Dougal stuffed the sopping bread into his mouth, wiped the drips on the table with his sleeve, and waited for his father to thunder into the cottage.

But Da came in quietly and didn't slam the door. He didn't say much and he had a strange look on his face, like he was inside his head and not in the cottage at all. Had Mam noticed, or Flora? Dougal caught Maggie's eye. She knew something was going on.

Later that night, Dougal lay in his bed listening to the north wind whistling through the cracks around the door. He shivered under his blanket and wished more heat from the fire would reach his corner. His feet were cold and even curled up in a ball he couldn't get warm, couldn't get to sleep.

He watched the shadow patterns flickering and dancing over the dark walls. Mam rocked in her chair by the fire with his baby sister in her arms. Da paced round the room. They were talking in quiet voices. It was just a murmuring of conversation. Dougal wasn't really listening, until he heard the words "New World."

Dougal frowned. *What did Da just say?*

"Leaving our homeland's a mighty painful decision," said Mam. She spoke slowly, as if it hurt even saying the words. "We can never come back."

Dougal bolted upright. *New World? Never come back?* What were they talking about?

"Aye," said Da. "I know. But we're all but starving here, and it's not going to get any better. How can it, when all our money goes on rent and taxes?" He threw a peat brick onto the fire, making it hiss and spark. "Morag, you should have heard John Ross. He's become the agent for a vast area of land in the New World. He said it's being divided up into farms. And they are giving them away free to anyone who wants to go and farm them. Imagine, Morag, our very own farm. No landlords. Just us working for ourselves. Being our own masters."

Da's voice got louder and faster as he spoke. "They're even calling the place Nova Scotia. That means New Scotland! And they'll provide supplies for a whole year to get us started."

"You know what they say about things sounding too good to be true?" said Mam. There was a snap in her voice.

"John Ross is a local man, he wouldn't see us wronged," Da shot back.

Mam's chair creaked as she rocked back and forth, back and forth. Dougal couldn't quite see her face so he leaned forward. As he did, some of the pebbles he'd collected for his slingshot fell out of his jacket pocket and clattered onto the floor.

Da spun round to face Dougal's bunk. "Dougal! Are you awake? Did you hear what we were saying?"

Dougal climbed out of bed and walked slowly over to his Da. He wasn't sure if he was in trouble or not. "I sort of heard some of it," he admitted, "but I don't understand. What are you talking about? Are we going to the New World?"

Without answering Dougal's question, Da went over to Mam's screen of drying herbs, ducked underneath, and dragged out the old weathered box he kept hidden there. From it he pulled out a length of plaid and loosely wound it round his waist, draping one end over his shoulder. Then he put on his war bonnet. Dougal hadn't seen his father dressed like this before. He looked so proud and seemed to stand taller.

"This is what I'm talking about, son," he said. "It's about living free. In our New Scotland, there'll be no English making up the rules and stopping me wearing the colours of my clan." Da turned towards Mam. His voice cracked. "What do you say, Morag…shall we go?"

Sparks shot up from the fire as Dougal held his breath, waiting for Mam's answer. It was so long coming, he began to think the sun would be up before she replied.

"My heart will break leaving the Highlands," she said at last. "But we have four hungry children to feed. If it's as good as Mr. Ross says, then of course we must go."

Da went and put his arms round her. "Our homeland's inside us," he said softly. "It's coming too."

Dougal's head was in a spin, and his heart felt like it was about to thump clean out of his chest. Da was going to take them to a country so far away that they could never come back. He needed to think about this, but his eyelids were suddenly too droopy to stay open.

"Go back to bed, Dougal," said Mam, gently. "We'll talk some more in the morning."

As they ate their porridge the next morning, Da told the whole family about the plan to go to Nova Scotia, in the Americas. First there would be a long sea voyage to the new country. Then the hard work would begin, building a cottage and planting the first crop on their very own farm.

Dougal leapt up from the bench with a great hoot. The thought of sailing across the ocean on one of the ships he'd seen from a distance was an adventure too exciting to imagine. Da laughed. Mam smiled but her eyes looked sad. Flora and Maggie looked from Mam to Da, and from Da to Mam, and didn't seem to know whether to be happy or sad.

"I'm going to book our passage before Mam has a chance to change her mind," said Da, with a wink. "Come, Dougal, we're going into town." Lately, Da had plodded about like his boots were made of stone, but today Dougal's twelve-year-old legs had to break into a run just to keep up.

While his father went to see John Ross, Dougal wandered about the village. He wondered if the town in Nova Scotia would be like this one, or if it would be completely different. Maybe there would be no town at all. He stopped to watch the blacksmith hammering a red-hot piece of metal into shape. *Our town can be any shape we like*, he thought. The excitement of it all made his heart spin.

"And what's making you so happy?" said a young man coming up to the forge. He was bony thin, with long dark curls tied back in a tail. His coat was torn and his breeks had been patched many times. He swung an odd-shaped bundle off his back and onto the ground.

"My Da's taking us right across the ocean, to the other side of the world," said Dougal, still not quite believing the words he was saying.

"Seems a lot of crofters are packing up and leaving," said the man. "I'm Johnny Mackay," he added. "I'd go myself if I had money for the passage. I've just the clothes on my back and my bagpipes."

The last word came out very quietly and Dougal wasn't quite sure he'd heard it right. "You have bagpipes?" he said.

"Keep your voice down," said Johnny Mackay, looking nervously over his shoulder.

Dougal had never seen bagpipes before, but he'd heard many a grand tale of pipers leading their clans into battle. As he looked at the blanket-wrapped bundle lying on the ground between them, a knowing smile crept over his face. "They're in there, aren't they?

Johnny dipped his head in the slightest of nods.

"Can I see them?" asked Dougal, keeping his voice low. "I swear I won't tell a single soul."

Johnny hesitated and glanced around. "A quick look. Come, we'll be out of sight over there." He led the way behind a huge boulder. Squatting down in the tall grasses, he carefully untied his blanket. The bagpipes weren't much to look at. They consisted of several long reed pipes tied together with braided hemp cords and a bag made out of leather. It was a dull grey-brown colour and had an odd musky smell. Dougal didn't care. He was too busy wondering what battles they'd been in and who'd played them. He lightly touched the smooth skin bag. It felt like the forbidden instrument would burn his fingers if his hand stayed on it too long, or else it would somehow mark him, so everyone could see he'd done something he shouldn't.

"They were my grandfather's," said Johnny, quickly rewrapping the bagpipes to get them out of sight again. "You should have heard him. Even the mountains seemed to listen when he played. He used to call me Wee Johnny Piper, 'cos I loved the pipes as much as he did." He stood and slung the bundle of pipes back over his shoulder. "But things change. I'm not so little anymore, and these pipes are all I have left of my grandfather."

"You must be really sad, now he's gone," said Dougal. He wished he'd known even one of his grandfathers, but they'd both been killed at the terrible Battle of Culloden. Da had told him how losing this battle had changed everything for the Highlanders. There were now severe penalties for wearing tartans, and playing the bagpipes was totally forbidden.

"Aye, I do miss Grandfather, but it's not only his passing that troubles me. See, when bagpipes were banned, Grandfather worried that as time passed, no one would know how to play them anymore." Johnny Piper heaved a deep sigh. "So on his deathbed, I promised I'd teach at least one other person to play."

Dougal's face scrunched into a frown. "That's a difficult promise to keep," he said.

"It surely is. It's hard enough finding places to play where I won't be heard. Teaching someone else…well, we'd both be in danger, and so would the pipes."

"I don't understand why bagpipes are banned anyway," said Dougal, shrugging his shoulders. "It doesn't make sense to me. Music can't hurt anyone."

"The English call them an 'instrument of war.'" Johnny Piper spat out the words like Da did every time he mentioned the English.

Dougal thought for a moment. "You've got to come to New Scotland, you've just got to. Da says we can make our own rules. You'll be able to play all you want and teach someone else to play, just like you promised."

"If only it was that easy," said Johnny Piper.

"There's my father now," said Dougal, as Da and a tall, smartly dressed man emerged from a building opposite the blacksmith's. "I'll tell him about your bagpipe problem. He'll think of something."

"No," said Johnny Piper, grabbing Dougal's arm. "Nobody must know about my bagpipes. My heart would break if they were taken from me and destroyed."

"I swore I wouldn't tell anyone and I won't," said Dougal. "Not even Ruari, and he's my best friend."

"Thanks," said Johnny Piper. "I know I can trust you."

"Dougal," called Da from across the square.

"I've got to go now," said Dougal. "Don't worry, I'll think of a plan." He ran over and stood next to his father.

"Mr. Ross, this is my son, Dougal."

"Pleased to meet you, sir," said Dougal.

John Ross looked Dougal up and down. "A fine young boy, Mr. Cameron," he said without actually saying anything to Dougal. "You'll be pioneers in a brave new land. What an amazing opportunity for your family. Well I'll bid you good day. I know we both have much to attend to."

John Ross pivoted on his heels and went back into his office.

"Goodbye, Mr. Ross, and thank you," called Da. He turned to Dougal, and with a smile, patted his jacket pocket. "Well, son, I've got our tickets. Our passage is booked on the *Hector*. That's the name of the ship that we will take to Nova Scotia. Let's get off home and show them to your Mam."

Da seemed to be smiling from the top of his head to the tips of his toenails. He didn't walk, he bounced. Dougal couldn't remember when he'd last seen his Da so happy. As they turned onto the road leading home, Dougal looked back at Johnny Piper and waved.

Johnny Piper waved back, and sauntered off in the opposite direction.

~~

The next day, Dougal helped his Da make a sturdy sea chest. "Whatever we can fit into this box is coming with us. The rest must go."

"Everything we own in one little box!" exclaimed Mam.

"Aye, and the first thing that's going in is my plaid. I'll need space for my tools too."

"Well I'm not leaving without my grandmother's herbal book," said Mam, crossing her arms. "If that's not coming, neither am I."

With a smile, Dougal left them arguing. The only thing he owned was his slingshot.

CHAPTER 3

AS THE COOL, WET SPRING GAVE WAY TO warmer days, Dougal couldn't help noticing how sad Mam looked as, piece by piece, their home was sold or given away. "Don't worry, Morag, I'll make you another one when we get to New Scotland," said Da every time something went out the door. This dark, cloudy morning it was Mam's precious rocking chair—the very last thing to be sold.

Dougal helped Da manoeuvre the chair, with its awkward sticking-out rockers, through the narrow doorway. Thunder rumbled in the distance and Dougal could sense the restlessness in the cows and horses grazing at the back of the croft. The animals didn't like thunder. A horse over the way caught Dougal's attention. It was rearing its head.

"Concentrate on what you're doing," said Da sternly as they staggered across the village clearing, the heavy piece of furniture suspended between them.

"Stop," yelped Dougal. "I need to put it down for a minute, my finger's pinched."

"Can't stop now," said Da. "It's going to pour any minute."

A streak of lightning flashed across the sky, followed instantly by a sharp crack of thunder. A horse shrieked. "Watch out!" yelled a crofter.

The warning came too late. The frightened horse bolted, knocking Da and Dougal to the ground in its petrified gallop.

Dougal picked himself up. "You all right, Da?"

His father didn't move.

Crofters dropped what they were doing and rushed over. Mam ran out with Wee Mary in her arms. She thrust the baby at Dougal and dropped to her knees beside Da's still body. A neighbour knelt and put his hand on Mam's shoulder. "His head hit that rock. I'm so terribly, terribly sorry, Morag."

All the colour drained from Mam's face. "Angus," she cried. "You can't leave us, not now."

"Make him better, Mam. You make everybody better," pleaded Dougal. "I'll fetch your bag of herbs." Mam's cries became a wail and the womenfolk gently led her home.

Dougal stood in the pouring rain clutching Wee Mary, trying desperately to understand what had just happened.

～

The rest of the day passed in a blur. A simple coffin was brought into the house with Da's body laid inside. Flora and Maggie decorated it with bunches of heather. Neighbours brought food. But Dougal, who was always hungry, couldn't swallow a single mouthful.

Dusk came. The neighbours left. Mam lit a candle. "Tonight I will sit with your father and tomorrow we will bury him," she said in a flat voice. "Go to bed, children."

"I'll stay up too," said Dougal, but he soon fell into an exhausted sleep on the floor beside his Da.

The next day, a mournful bell announced the funeral. Parson Brown, his robes flapping like the wings of an old crow, led the procession across a cold empty field to the burying place. Dougal knew the sound of dirt thudding onto his Da's coffin would stay in his head forever.

Simple food was spread on tables for the wake. All the villagers came to show their respect and comfort Mam.

"Sorry about your Da," said Ruari.

"Me too," said Dougal, and edged away. He didn't want to talk to anybody but as he drifted around he couldn't help hearing the whispers. "Poor souls, what will they do now?"

~~

Dougal woke the next day to the hush of the bare house. Mam and his sisters were still asleep. The neighbours were gone, the coffin was gone, the table and chairs were gone, and his big, loud Da was gone. All that was left was Mam's cookpot, the shawls and quilts on their beds, and the half-filled sea chest. It sat by the wall, where Da had left it. Nothing had been added and nothing taken out.

When Mam and his sisters got up they moved around like ghosts. Even the baby's cries seemed quieter. Dougal watched the door, certain his Da would suddenly reappear and it had all been a bad dream.

The sun rose and set and every misery-filled hour in-between seemed to last a week. Dougal didn't know losing someone could hurt so much or that he'd feel so empty. It was like part of him had gone missing and would never come back.

Another day went by then another. All the while the pain he felt inside got worse.

〜

"Dougal!" Ruari cried, coming through the sunlight and into the gloom of the croft.

"Go away," said Dougal, in a flat voice.

"Want to climb Mowry's Crag?" asked Ruari, looking at his feet. Dougal knew Ruari's mam had sent him over, and Ruari didn't really want to spend time with him, even if it got him out of picking stones. Death had that effect on people. No one knew what to say because there was nothing to say, nothing that made any sense.

Ruari shuffled from one foot to another, making a hollow in the dirt floor, as he waited for Dougal's answer.

All Dougal wanted to do was sit in the shadows. He barely got through his daily chores. The fire in the middle of the croft had gone out. Da would never allow that to happen, but Mam didn't seem to care. "No," he said, at last. "I'm the man of the family now. I can't play anymore."

"I understand," said Ruari, and with a sad look on his face, quietly slipped out of the door.

After a while, Dougal wandered down to the shore. He picked up a large pebble and hurled it into the waves. It landed with an angry splash in the grey water. Pebble after pebble met the same fate. Someday they were meant to leave for the harbour at Loch Broom to get the ship taking them to New Scotland. What would happen now?

Dougal dragged himself back home. Mam was sitting outside rocking Wee Mary. "So! Are we going to New Scotland or not?" he demanded.

Mam let out a long sigh. Her eyes were pink and puffy and a tear slid down her cheek. She brushed it away with an attempt at a laugh. "I thought I was all cried out, seems I'm not. I don't know what we're going to do, Dougal."

Dougal didn't mean to be mad at Mam. He just felt mad at everything and everybody. He was mad at Da for dying and he was especially mad at the dumb horse for causing the accident.

"Let's talk about what to do next," he said, puffing himself up. After all, he was the man of the family now. It actually felt good to think about something other than feeling sad and angry.

"Yes, let's think about the future," said Mam. She smiled through her watery eyes. "Well, we can't stay here because Da gave in our notice and new tenants will be moving into our croft."

"Ruari's Da might let me work for him," said Dougal, "and the village would help us out."

"I know they would," said Mam. "They've hearts as big as the Highlands. But they've barely enough to feed their own families. We can't add to their burden."

"Any other suggestions?"

"Your uncle in town would take us in. He'd say it was his duty. You'd work for him of course, and, knowing my brother, he'd try and find me a new husband as quickly as possible."

Dougal's face went tight and he shook his head. "Oh no," he said. "Definitely no. I do not want a new Da."

Wee Mary had fallen asleep. Dougal followed Mam as she went inside and laid the baby down on the bed. Then she went over to the sea chest. "All your Da's dreams are in this wooden box." She opened the lid and pulled out

Da's plaid. Dougal took the long length of rough, woven cloth from her. It had belonged to his grandfather. The colours were faded and it had been darned, and patched many times.

Da's tartan made Dougal think of Johnny Piper's grandfather. He'd had a dream and passed that dream on to Johnny. Now Johnny was trying to find a way to teach someone how to play a forbidden instrument. A thought bounced into Dougal's head. Da had had an important dream too. Could Dougal be like Johnny Piper, and make Da's dream come true?

"Mam," he said, "Da wanted us to live free on our own farm more than anything in the whole world. He told me that when we went to buy our passage. The tickets are bought. Let's make his dream come true and live free on our own farm just like he planned."

Mam looked at Dougal. Two pink patches appeared on her cheeks and her eyes took on a strange sparkle.

"You really think we should go to New Scotland on our own?"

Dougal nodded.

"Oh, Dougal, do you really think we can?"

"I know we can."

"We'll have to work all the hours God sends, and more."

"I'm a hard worker," said Dougal.

"But you're only twelve years old."

"I'm growing."

Mam sucked thoughtfully on her bottom lip for a moment, then a nervous, excited expression spread slowly over her face. "Folk are going to say I've no more sense than my old cookpot. But...let's do it, Dougal. Let's go to Nova Scotia."

Dougal threw his arms around his mother.

"What's all the hugging?" said Flora, coming into the house with Maggie trotting behind her.

"We're still going to the Americas," said Dougal. A shiver of excitement rushed through his body as he said the words. It pushed away some of his sadness. But he was a little scared too. He couldn't imagine a strange new life without his Da.

"If we're going we must hurry," said Mam. "We should have left already. There's a hundred things to do before we go. Dougal, fetch Da's mallet, his knife, and any other tools you think we might need."

Mam packed her best shawl, her herbal book, and a bag of dried herbs. Just before Dougal closed the lid, she slipped in a bunch of lavender and heather. "It will make the chest smell good and we can plant the seeds in New Scotland. We'll wear all our clothes and put our quilts and blankets round our shoulders. You can each bring one special thing," said Mam. "But you must carry it."

Dougal flexed the loop on his slingshot. "This is what I'm bringing," he said. "It fits in my pocket."

"I'm bringing Dolly," said Maggie.

"Like anything could get Dolly out of your arms," teased Dougal. "What are you bringing, Flora?"

Flora thought for a moment. "My dancing feet," she said, at last. "And they're attached so I won't have to carry them."

"I like that choice," said Mam. She wrapped whatever food they had left in a wet cloth and put it with their cups and bowls in her big cookpot, which was most definitely coming too.

The next day they were ready to leave. A neighbour with a handcart offered to help them bring their belongings to Loch Broom. After loading in Da's sea chest, Mam's cookpot, and the quilts and blankets from their beds, they started their journey.

"Stop! Wait!" said Dougal. "I haven't said goodbye to Ruari."

"Be quick then," said Mam. "We really do have to get going. We don't want to miss the boat."

Dougal found Ruari hoeing between the rows of turnips. He stopped work and walked over to Dougal. "Guess you're off then," said Ruari.

In a heart-stopping moment, Dougal realized he'd never see Ruari again, not ever. Things were happening faster than he could think.

"It won't be the same here without you," continued Ruari. "But every time I see a ship on the horizon, I'm going to think of you and all the adventures you're having."

"I'm going to miss you too," said Dougal, "and all of this."

"I don't think so. Your turnips will be twice the size of ours and you'll never be hungry again."

"Maybe." Dougal went up and hugged Ruari then ran off to join Mam. If he stayed any longer he'd start bawling.

Dougal looked back at the small stone cottage that had been his home. He felt like a wisp of thistledown spinning into the sky, not knowing where the wind would take it, or where it would land.

"Don't look back," said Mam, putting a hand on his shoulder. "Look forward."

CHAPTER 4

IT WAS EARLY EVENING WHEN THEY REACHED
the little harbour at Loch Broom. Dougal had never
seen so many people in one place before. Families were
camped out in makeshift shelters along the river, around
the glen, and all the way down to the harbour. Wafts of
smoke from the cook fires drifted up into the blue sky.

Flora immediately dropped what she was carrying and danced away, her dark curls bouncing along
behind.

"Flora, stay near," Mam called after her. The neighbour unloaded our sea chest off his cart. "Godspeed to
you all," he said, patting Mam warmly on the shoulder.
"And good luck. You'll surely need it." With a worried
shake of his head, he turned for home.

"Where's our ship?" asked Dougal.

Mam looked towards the loch. "I was wondering that
myself. It can't have gone or all these people wouldn't
be here."

"It's been delayed, Mrs. Cameron." A tall, smartly dressed man walked over to join them. It was John Ross. "I'm deeply sorry for your loss."

"Thank you," said Mam, putting on the fancy voice she only used for Parson Brown. "As you see we decided to proceed as planned."

"You won't regret it. I assure you."

"And when will our ship be here, Mr. Ross?"

The agent looked heavenward. "It's out of our hands, dear lady," he said. "Rest assured it will be here soon as it can."

Dougal didn't really like this man. He had a snooty sort of smile.

"You're the last to arrive," added John Ross. "As you can see we provided shelters, but they are all taken. Still, it's a warm night and no sign of rain. You'll be fine under the stars."

"I'm sure we will," said Mam. Her fancy voice had turned huffy. "As long as the good weather continues. Come, Dougal. We have to make camp."

Dougal followed his Mam to a spot by a bright yellow broom bush. "This will have to do," she said with an exasperated sigh. They spread the quilts on the springy heather. While Mam nursed the baby, Dougal collected some dry peat and lit a small fire. He then fetched some water from the river and set it to boil.

When their meal was ready, Flora came bouncing up and sat still just long enough to eat her potatoes and bannock before skipping off to join her new friends. Five-year-old Maggie lay her head on Mam's knee and hugged Dolly in her arms. Dougal went off to explore.

He started at the water's edge where some lads were skipping pebbles. Picking up a flat piece of flint stone, he squatted down and, with a twist of his fingers, sent it skimming over the still waters of the loch. It bounced four times.

"That the best you can do, Poxy-face?" scoffed one of the lads. He skimmed his rock. It only bounced twice. His friends guffawed. Another boy matched Dougal's four.

"My record's seven," boasted Dougal, ignoring the taunt he hadn't heard for a while. But before he could throw again, a pair of tired old oxen, pulling an overladen wagon, snorted up to the water's edge.

"Get out the bleedin' way," bellowed the red-faced driver, jumping down from the box. He shook his fists and the rock skippers scattered in all directions. Dougal slipped the sharp stone he'd been holding into his pocket, then ran off and hid behind a line of large water barrels.

When his breathing had slowed, Dougal snuck his head out a little ways. There was no sign of the other lads and the man was now shouting at someone else. Dougal came out of hiding and continued exploring. He poked round the crates in front of a makeshift store selling supplies but the only thing of interest was a family of mice helping themselves to some spilled oats. He left them to it and climbed inside a huge coil of rope until he was chased off from there too.

Standing on his toes, Dougal looked out over the water. If he could get up a bit higher, he'd be able to see much farther and he might even be able to spot their ship. He remembered a rocky crag they'd passed at the entrance to the harbour. He'd get a good view from atop that. He jogged back to it, then climbed as nimbly as a mountain goat to a high ledge. Below him he could see the tiny camps and busy, ant-sized people.

Dougal's eyes travelled slowly upwards across the blueness to where the sea met the sky.

Somewhere out of sight over the horizon was New Scotland. But where was the ship that would take them there? He moved his eyes back and forth over the water. There was no sign of a ship.

He loved being high above the world. On the ground his insides were a mush of excitement and sadness. He was the man of the family now, and he had to be strong like his Da, but how would he know what to do when everything would be so different? Up here he was able to leave those feelings behind. The July sunlight was a deep gold and would stay that way for a few more hours. Dougal so hoped he'd love the new Scotland as much as he loved the real Scotland.

A bald eagle flapped by. As Dougal's eyes followed her to her nest, he noticed a dark speck on the horizon. It hadn't been there a minute ago. With his hands shielding his eyes, Dougal squinted at the speck. He was sure it was getting bigger. He kept watching. It was definitely coming nearer, and he could just about make out the squares of the sails and the dark line of its hull.

It must be their ship!

He clambered down and ran all the way back to the harbour yelling on the top of his voice, "The *Hector*'s coming. The *Hector*'s coming!"

The settlers on the bank heard his cry. "The *Hector*'s coming," they repeated to each other as they hurried to the water's edge.

John Ross heard the words and pushed his way through the crowd. He pulled a spyglass from his pocket and scanned the horizon. "Aye!" he said, at last. "It is a Dutch brig. That is indeed the *Hector*. We'll be leaving tomorrow."

A great cheer went up from the crowd. People started laughing and hugging each other. Dougal noticed some tears too. "The *Hector*'s coming, the *Hector*'s coming" sang the children dancing in and out. Dougal went to find his Mam and saw Johnny Piper standing at the edge of the glen.

"You found the money for your passage?" Dougal cried, running over to the tall, thin figure.

"'Fraid not," said Johnny. "Just came to see you off."

Dougal's face fell. "I so wanted you to come."

"Me too. It's going to be a great adventure."

Dougal wasn't so sure anymore. Now that leaving was becoming real, all he could think of was his old home. He scuffed the ground with his boots. Then he looked up at Johnny Piper. "Play your pipes," he said. "I've never heard the sound of bagpipes. If you don't play I might never ever hear them in my whole life."

"It's dangerous," said Johnny Piper. He looked around at all the families getting ready for their new lives. The air hummed with excitement and anticipation. "But I don't care," he said with a grin. "I'm going to play anyway. Keep a look out for me, Dougal. I may have to run."

Dougal's face lit up then went deadly serious. He puffed out his chest. "I'll watch out for you. No one will take your pipes while I'm around."

Johnny Piper assembled the ancient instrument, then he wedged the narrow skin bag under his arm, arranged the drone pipes over his shoulder, and blew steadily down the small pipe he'd tucked into the corner of his mouth. As he marched forward, he gently squeezed the bag and a deep thrum filled the glen.

Everyone stopped what they were doing and looked at the ragged piper. Even the children were still. The sounds vibrated through Dougal's body. He couldn't believe an instrument could growl and soar and dance all at the same time. The sound was so big it filled the glen.

Johnny played an old familiar song, then, without stopping, began another. Feet started tapping and folk began dancing. Hands held high, they spun with skirts flying and faces beaming. As the sun slowly sank in the sky, the dancing continued, with everyone joining in. Flora dragged shy Maggie and Dolly into a circle with the other children and, holding hands, they skipped round the piper. Mam swung Wee Mary in her arms.

Dougal didn't move from Johnny Piper's side. His eyes darted about the crowds, looking for anyone who might arrest Johnny or take his pipes. No one looked suspicious. Everyone was too busy having a good time. As Dougal clapped and stamped along to the music, he knew he wanted to be a piper more than anything else in the whole world. But it was just a dream. There'd be no bagpipes in New Scotland.

The *Hector* grew closer, and the shape of the ship was clear to everyone. "The pipes are calling it in," said Mam with a laugh. *That's her first real smile since Da died*, thought Dougal and it made him feel good.

Dusk settled on Loch Broom. John Ross signalled to Johnny Piper to finish the song. "The night is short and a long day lies ahead," said John Ross. "Time to get some sleep. Good night to you all."

Dougal watched Johnny pack away his bagpipes as the settlers gathered up their tired children and shuffled back to their camps.

"That was good playing," said Mam. "You're so young too."

"I'm nineteen years and I've been playing ever since I could stand up. My grandfather was my teacher."

"You have to come with us," said Dougal. "You just have to."

CHAPTER 5

WEE MARY WAS THE FIRST TO WAKE THE NEXT morning. Dougal remembered, with a pang, how Da used to say her cries were better than a rooster's cock-o-doodle-do for telling the family the day had begun. Dougal opened his eyes, surprised at first to find he was sleeping in the open. Two things came into his mind as he lazily watched Mam tend to his baby sister. The first was seeing what their ship looked like, and the second was finding a way to get Johnny Piper on-board.

"Mam, could Johnny Piper use Da's ticket?"

Mam shook her head. "I returned it."

"Of course," said Dougal. "I should have thought." He stood up. "I'm going to see the *Hector*."

Other passengers were already at the water's edge, staring out at a very old ship anchored just offshore. Dougal had never seen a ship close up, but he hadn't imagined any ship looking as squat and ugly as this old hulk. The vessel was flat at both ends, with a short raised

deck at the back. It had two large masts, a long spar sticking out at the front, and a small mast at the back. Dirty
grey sails hung in droopy bundles along the crosspieces.

Maybe this isn't our ship, thought Dougal. Theirs would
come sailing over the horizon at any moment. But Mam
had taught him his letters and "Hector" was written
clearly on the back of the black hull.

"I don't believe it," said Mam, coming up to join him.
"We paid good money for our passage. That ship's a
decrepit old wreck, and it's so small."

Dougal looked at all the folk camped out in Loch
Broom and then at the *Hector* then back at the people.
How were they all going to fit? "At least it's got guns,"
he said, imagining a mighty sea battle.

"Look closer, laddie," said a bristly old man, his white
hair hanging like a curtain around his head. "The gun
windows are painted on to fool American privateers.
There are no guns."

The complaints and grumbles grew louder as more
passengers came to see the vessel that was to take them
to the other side of the world.

"It doesn't look seaworthy to me," said a woman, stopping to stand beside them.

"And it's not much bigger than my cottage," said
Mam. "*Is mise* Morag," she said, meeting the woman's
eyes. "My name is Morag."

"*Is mise* Isobel. *Tha mi toilichte do coinneachadh.* I'm pleased
to meet you. My husband, Malcolm, and I are travelling to
the New World. We want a better life for our new baby."
She stroked her rounded belly. "Of course he's not due to
make an appearance for another few months."

"Mam's helped birth lots of babies," boasted Dougal.

"But I'm sure my skills won't be needed on this voyage,"

said Mam, shooting Dougal a 'please be quiet' look. "I understand the voyage will take about four or five weeks, so your baby will be the first birth in New Scotland."

Isobel's shy titters were interrupted by the appearance of John Ross. Isobel grabbed on to Morag as the crowd swarmed by, on their way to confront the agent.

"Ross, we want an explanation!" shouted the old man who knew about the painted-on gun windows. "This boat isn't seaworthy enough to make it out of the loch, let alone take all these folk across the ocean."

With a lot of fist waving the crowd cried out in agreement, adding more loud complaints of their own.

"Nothing to worry about, I assure you," said John Ross. "Everything is fine, we'll be on our way very soon."

"Look," said Dougal, "there's a longboat from the *Hector*."

All eyes turned towards the water. Pushing his way through the commotion of angry settlers, John Ross strode towards the imposing-looking man in the three-cornered hat who'd just jumped ashore.

"Captain Spiers," he said, holding out his hand in greeting, "I'm John Ross, the agent."

The Captain ignored it. "Mr. Ross, I assume all is ready for the voyage. We are well behind schedule. I trust you will inform your employers that I'm exceedingly unhappy about this. We should have left a month ago. Late summer hurricanes have a habit of creeping up from the South."

Before John Ross could babble out any excuses, the Captain turned to the Bosun. "Don't just stand there, man, I want those stores on-board, and be quick about it." He looked around. "And where are the rest of the supplies and the extra water?"

"There's enough here for a five-week voyage," said John Ross. "That's what I was told to supply."

"You seriously think we'll get there in that time!" exclaimed Captain Spiers, shaking his head in disbelief. "The westerly winds will be pushing against us every inch of the way. We'll be on half rations before we even begin."

At this, the crowd went strangely quiet. "What's he saying?" asked one of the settlers.

"Don't know," said another. "I can't understand English. Seems he's the captain, and he doesn't look happy."

Dougal went and found Mam. They did know how to speak English. Da had taught them the harsh sounding language as they sat round the fire on winter evenings, telling them it was important to know what the enemy was saying.

"Mam, is it going to be all right?" asked Dougal.

Her face had gone rather pale but she smiled at him. "I'm sure everything will be fine. The Captain's just in a rush to be off, that's all. I don't think he's a very patient man. But he looks like a good captain."

Dougal wasn't completely convinced. He squeezed to the front of the crowd so he could hear some more.

Captain Spiers was surveying the scene around the harbour and giving orders. "We'll start taking the families on-board as soon as the stores are loaded. I'll need everyone packed up and in line with their belongings. Is that clear, Mr. Ross?"

"Extremely clear," said John Ross, through gritted teeth. He stomped off, barking instructions as he went.

Mam and Dougal hurried back to their camp and found Johnny Piper rocking Wee Mary with one hand and tickling Maggie into a bundle of giggles with the other. Flora was still asleep. "Wake up, Flora," said

Dougal. "We've got to get on-board." Flora snuffled and turned over.

"Leave her be," said Mam. "It was a very late night. We'll have breakfast first. No need to rush, we're going to be on that ship for a very long time. Get the fire going, Dougal."

Mam made a big pot of oatmeal and invited Johnny Piper to have breakfast with them. Dougal took his bowl to where he could watch the longboat going back and forth between the *Hector* and the shore, loading supplies for the voyage.

He ran back to Johnny Piper. "Can you swim?" he asked, breathlessly. "The *Hector*'s not very far out. You could swim round the back and climb aboard. Everyone will be looking this way so no one'd see you."

Johnny Piper shook his head. "Not a stroke."

"Me neither," said Dougal with a shrug. He returned to his observation post. The first families were standing in line now. He noticed how their names were being checked off a list. There was a lot of confusion and many women were holding babies. Maybe if Johnny Piper draped Mam's shawl over his head and carried Wee Mary, in all the kerfuffle he might just be able to get on-board with no one recognizing him.

"Leave me out of this," said Mam after Dougal explained his plan. "It's dishonest and I want nothing to do with it. And no way am I letting our baby out of my arms."

Flora squinted at Johnny and giggled. "You'd look funny as a girl."

"I would indeed," said Johnny Piper. He stood up. "I'll no' be dressing up like a lass. Thank you for the breakfast, ma'am. It's time I was on my way."

"Don't go," said Dougal. "You don't have to dress up. I'll think of something else."

Johnny Piper ruffled Dougal's hair, which made Dougal feel like a silly wee boy. "Godspeed. I'll be thinking of you all."

"Good luck to you too and my heart thanks you for playing to us last night," said Mam.

Johnny Piper picked up his bundle of bagpipes and left. Dougal wanted to run after him but Mam caught his arm. "We have lots to do before we go on-board. Dougal, wash out my cookpot in the river. Flora, take this bag and fill it with crowberries, you know the ones. Maggie, sit here and watch your sister. I need to gather some herbs. Then we'll all have a good wash in the river, pack up our camp, and get in line."

CHAPTER 6

DOUGAL FELT LIKE A HERRING IN A FISHING net, squished on the longboat floor with the baggage and the other children. The baby fussed as Mam slid along the bench to make room for the old man Dougal had been talking to earlier. His wife sat down next to him. Dougal didn't think there was room for any more people, but they were ordered to squeeze up, and two more families and their belongings were hustled on-board.

"Ridiculous," growled the old man. "This boat's so overcrowded, we'll all be drowned before we even get on-board."

"Shhh now," said his wife. "I'm sure they know what they're doing."

"Move over, Maggie, you're squashing me," whined Flora, elbowing her sister.

Maggie's face crumpled. "I wwwant to gggo hhh-home," she sobbed, pressing her wet face into Mam's skirt.

"Don't cry, Maggie, this is the exciting bit," said Dougal, stretching up to get a better view.

It was late afternoon and it had been a long, hot, boring day waiting as the longboat went back and forth between the harbour and the *Hector*. Dougal had felt very sullen after Johnny Piper left, but now that he was sitting in the longboat, the excitement was back, tickling his insides.

The longboat cut through the choppy little waves of the loch and in a few short minutes arrived at the ship that was to be their home for the next few weeks. The crew stowed the oars and the longboat gently bumped against the side of the *Hector*. The passengers scrambled to get their belongings, causing the longboat to rock alarmingly.

"Sit down, or you'll have us all in the drink!" bellowed a crew member. "Wait your turn. We'll get you on-board one family at a time."

"Hull's completely rotten," grumbled the old man in a voice loud enough for everyone in the longboat to hear. "I could tell that from a mile away. Up close, it's worse than I thought."

"Just needs a coat of paint, Hugh dear," said his wife.

"Coat of paint be danged. Ship's rotting away, I tell you."

"The deck's awful high," said Mam, ignoring the old man's opinions. "I don't know how I'm going to get three young'uns and all our baggage right up there."

"I'll help you up, Mam," said Dougal. He was itching to climb the rough strut ladder nailed to the side of the hull.

As he spoke, a large barrel that had been cut in half was lowered and a woman and two little girls climbed inside. Swaying madly, it was hauled up to the deck. "See, that's how it's done," said Dougal. "I'll climb up and meet you at the top."

"Oh no," said Mam. "We're all staying together. I need you to help keep hold of Maggie and Flora. Where is Flora? She was right here a minute ago."

"Flora," called Mam.

Dougal stood up. "Flora! We're getting out now."

"She must be here somewhere," said Mam. "It's only a small boat."

Dougal looked under the seats and between the bundles of belongings. The other passengers started looking too. Flora had vanished.

"No!" cried Mam, covering her face with her hands. "Please! Please don't let her have fallen over the side."

"There she is," squealed Maggie, pointing Dolly's arm at the barrel rising up the side of the ship.

Flora, who'd climbed in with another family, was waving at them with a saucy grin on her face.

"That naughty girl," declared Mam, laughing and crying at the same time. "Dougal, quick up the ladder, catch her and don't let her out of your sight."

Climbing up the side of the rocking hull wasn't as easy as Dougal thought it would be. The footholds were narrow and it was hard to get a grip. A small chunk of wood came loose in his hand and fell into the water. Dougal scrambled onto the deck just as Flora was climbing out of the barrel. He pulled her aside. "You're in big trouble. You just wait until Mam gets here. You're going to get such a scolding."

"Oww! You're hurting me," said Flora.

Dougal loosened his grip, but didn't let go of his wriggling sister.

The ship was already chock-o-block full. As Dougal waited for Mam he couldn't help wondering if the ship would sink if any more people got on-board, or if the sails would be able to pull all this weight along. And what if it wasn't just the strut ladder that was rotten but the whole ship, just like the old man said? Would they disappear under the waves in the middle of the ocean?

At long last it was Mam and the girls' turn to ride the barrel up the side of the hull. Mam had tied the baby to her chest with her shawl, leaving her hands free to hang onto Maggie. A sailor helped them onto the deck and handed them their bundles. Dougal elbowed a path through the hubbub of angry settlers and screaming children to the hatchway leading down to the accommodations. He couldn't understand why everyone was so mad—until he climbed down the ladder.

The dark, vile-smelling, cavernous space was filled with crudely made wooden bunks. They were stacked three or four high and already cram-packed with settlers. There were no portholes and the only light came from smelly fish-oil lamps hung from the bulkheads. The only air came from the hatch they'd just climbed through.

Mam's face froze in horror as she took in the scene. "Heaven preserve us!" she exclaimed. "I can't think of words dreadful enough to describe all this."

"Move along," called a young sailor.

"Which bunks are ours?" asked Mam, shouting to be heard above the noise.

"Take your pick," he answered, then continued in a sing-song voice, "one bunk a family, five to a bunk."

Mam's mouth gaped open. "One bunk for five people! But they're barely two foot wide and there's not enough room to sit up in them. You expect us to live like this for weeks on end? We paid good money for our tickets. Look!" She angrily waved their tickets in his face. Dougal had never seen his mother this wild. It wasn't like her at all.

The young sailor ignored her and continued on, calling out the "one bunk a family" chant to the next people coming down the ladder.

"If only your Da was here," said Mam. "He wouldn't let them get away with this."

Dougal's heart sank into his scuffy boots. He was the man of the family now. He should be trying to make things right, but what was he meant to do? He looked about and saw that families with menfolk were being treated exactly the same.

"I'll find us a bunk," he said. That was something he could do.

"Excuse me, excuse me," Dougal cried, as he tried to edge his way through the bumping, shoving crowds filling the narrow gangways between the bunks. No one let him by so he got down on his hands and knees and squeezed between their legs until he found a gap and was able to stand up. Looking at each of the bunks in turn, he slowly pushed his way along the length of the ship. Seemed every bunk was already overflowing with people. Further and further away from the fresh air and the light he went.

Finally, at the very front of the ship, three levels off the ground, was an empty bunk. He climbed up and claimed it. "Mam!" he yelled at the top of his voice. "Mam, over here!" He waved and waved and his voice got hoarse shouting over the din. Eventually, Mam saw him and led Maggie and Flora over.

"This was all I could find," said Dougal, climbing down. "Will it do?"

"Not like we have any choice," Mam answered with a huff. "I heard the front is where you get the worst of the motion, but there's nothing to be done."

Wee Mary's cries were getting louder. She was hungry. So was Dougal.

The grouchy old man they'd been sitting next to in the longboat stuck his head out from a bunk across the way. "Can't you keep that dang baby quiet?"

Oh no, thought Dougal. *Not him again.*

Before Mam could answer, the man was yanked back into his bunk, and his wife stuck her head out. Dougal was glad to see that she had a kind face. "My name's Janet," the woman said. "We didn't get a chance to meet on the longboat. Now don't you take any notice of Hugh, the old curmudgeon will grumble about anything." She smiled at Wee Mary. "That's a bonny baby you have there. Now you let me know if I can do anything to help."

"Thank you, Janet," said Mam. "There's certainly a lot to grumble about. I don't know how we're going to get through the next few weeks. I really don't."

"It's going to take some courage, but we Scots have plenty of that. And we're used to hardship, aren't we, hen? We'll get through this."

"Yes, we will," said Mam, defiantly. She stuck out her chin. "Come on, girls, let's turn this bunk into a snug home for the voyage."

Dougal boosted Flora and Maggie up and they squirmed around, arranging the quilts and hanging up their own curtain.

"It's dark, but cozy," said Mam, bumping her head as she joined the girls in the bunk. "We'll do just fine here.

Pass out the bannock and the berries, Flora." She lay down to nurse Wee Mary.

"I'm going to take mine on deck," said Dougal. "I want to find out what's going on."

The deck was almost as crowded as the hold, but the air was fresh. Dougal breathed in the smell of the ocean and watched the seagulls swooping and shrieking above him. As he walked around, his eyes followed the ropes and halyards up the masts and he wondered what it would be like to climb way up there in a wild storm.

"Stowaway! Over here."

Dougal spun round to the direction of the shout. A thin, raggedly dressed man was dragged out from behind some water barrels.

"Get him off my ship," ordered the Captain.

"No!" shouted Dougal, pushing his way through to where the Captain was standing. "That's Johnny Piper."

CHAPTER 7

EVERYONE ON DECK STOPPED WHAT THEY WERE doing and gathered around. "It *is* the piper," said Old Hugh.

Johnny Piper's shoulders were shaking as he stood in front of the Captain. Dougal was trembling too, but he took a deep breath and stepped forward. "Please, sir," he said to the Captain, "let him stay. We need a piper in New Scotland."

"Aye! The piper has to come with us," said a settler. Others called out in agreement.

"Quiet," yelled the Captain as the clamour of voices got louder. "I insist on order aboard my ship."

John Ross stepped forward and held up his hand to quiet the crowd. "Captain, this voyage is going to be an extremely difficult time for these families. A piper will keep their spirits up. I advise you to let the piper stay."

"And who'll feed him?" snapped the Captain.

"We all will," chorused the settlers.

"Aye," said Old Hugh. "The sound of the pipes is worth more than a few scraps of food, and he's a mighty fine piper."

The Captain looked around at the faces of the settlers. "So be it," he said at last. A great cheer rose from the *Hector*'s deck and the Captain had to wait to finish what he was saying. "But when supplies run low, which they will, you'll rue the day you took on an extra mouth to feed." He turned to his crew. "Haul up the anchor. We've wasted enough time."

Johnny Piper let out a huge sigh of relief. "Thanks, Dougal. That water looks awful cold."

"How did you get on-board?"

"Easy, I helped a sailor carry a crate into the longboat. They all thought I was one of the crew."

Dougal laughed. "Never thought of that one."

To a chorus of commands, the discoloured sails jerked up the mast. The anchor was raised and the *Hector* started to move.

It seemed everyone was up on deck now. Dougal couldn't see over the forest of waving arms, so he climbed up onto the side, and with one elbow hooked through the rigging, leaned out over the water. He hadn't anybody to wave to, but he wanted to look at Scotland for as long as he possibly could. The wind whipped his hair and made his eyes sting.

Then Dougal's heart missed a beat and he nearly lost his grip. Through the salty spray he could see his Da waving to him from the shore. Dougal blinked hard to clear his blurry eyes. His Da was still there, getting smaller and smaller as the *Hector* pulled away from the shore.

"Stay with us, Da," he called, wildly waving his arm.

"Dougal Angus Cameron, get yourself back inside the ship this minute."

Dougal startled. He hadn't seen his mother come up on deck. He swung himself round and jumped down, still stunned at what he had seen. "Want to wave goodbye to Scotland, Maggie?"

The little girl nodded. Dougal squatted down so she could climb onto his shoulders. He wanted to know if she could see Da too, but she didn't say anything and Dougal didn't ask. He didn't tell Mam what he'd seen either.

The chords of a haunting lament drifted over the ship as the settlers continued to wave goodbye to their beloved homeland.

"'Flowers of the Forest,'" said a settler, wiping his eyes. "Piper's earned his passage already."

"Aye, that he has," said another.

The bright yellow broom bushes, which gave Loch Broom its name, faded into the distance as the *Hector* wove her way through the islands of the sea loch and out into the open Atlantic.

"*Cha till Mi tuille*," said Mam, with a sigh as deep as the loch. "We'll return no more."

"There'll be no more land until the Americas come into sight," declared the Captain.

"No more Da," sighed Dougal.

CHAPTER 8

THAT NIGHT, WRAPPED IN MAM'S OLD SHAWL, Dougal slept on the deck. It gave Mam and the girls more room and he didn't mind sleeping outside in the fresh air one bit. He wasn't the only one: the deck was dotted with bundled sleepers.

Dougal lay listening to the unfamiliar creaks and groans of the ancient hull. Weird shadows danced over the deck as the sailor on watch walked by with his oil lamp. Dougal's old life had ended but his new life hadn't begun yet. It was a very strange place to be. Had seeing his Da on the shore been a dream? Had it been Da's ghost? *Probably just an imagining*, thought Dougal as he drifted off to sleep.

Dawn came early and it looked like another fine day. Dougal went to pee over the side.

"Spit first," shouted the young sailor who'd shown them the bunks.

Dougal spat, and the glob blew right back in his face. The sailor slapped his sides and laughed like he'd never ever seen anything so funny in his whole life.

"Thanks, I think," said Dougal. He wiped his face, then walked across the deck and peed over the other side of the ship. While he was there, he took out the sharp flint he'd pocketed at Loch Broom and scratched a small notch on the top edge of the gunwale. He was going to do that every morning to count the days.

The sailor came over to join him. "Caught me out my first time," he said, still snickering. "Name's Samuel Miles but they calls me Smiley. Anything you want to know about the sea, you ask old Smiley here."

Smiley had a broad freckly face and hair that looked like a pitchfork of straw had landed on top of his head. He wasn't much older than Dougal, so Dougal couldn't see how he could possibly know much about anything. Smiley was holding a knotted rope attached to a metal cylinder. Dougal's eyebrows shot up in surprise as Smiley tossed the cylinder over the side.

"What did you do that for?"

"Keeping us from being shipwrecked," said Smiley, smugly.

Dougal's face twisted into a disbelieving frown. "If you and that frayed piece of rope are all that's keeping us from getting wrecked, we're in big trouble."

Smiley jiggled the wet rope, purposely splashing Dougal.

"Hey," laughed Dougal. "So, how exactly are you and your old rope going to save my life?"

"See those knots?" asked Smiley. Dougal leaned over the side of the ship and saw one knot after another disappearing under the waves. "Each one is a fathom.

Every morning I count how many knots went under the water. I'm really good at counting. Then I tell the Bosun and he tells the Captain and then the Captain knows how deep the water is under us. Clever, eh!"

"Stop yer slacking, you good-for-nothing lout," yelled the Bosun from across the other side of the ship. Smiley gave Dougal a lopsided grin.

"Best get back to work," said Smiley. Hand over hand he pulled up the rope, counting out loud, as the knots thudded back on-board.

"Interesting," said Dougal. Well, everything on the ship was interesting.

"See you later, Smiley." Dougal waved and went to find Mam and the girls.

He'd only taken a couple of steps down the hatch when the stink of the hold hit him in the face. The putrid mix of tar, urine, and vomit was far worse than the decomposing rat, heaving with maggots, that Dougal and Ruari had found in an outbuilding last spring. That smell had come from one place, but this stench was all around. He recognized Wee Mary's cries over all the groans and moans in the hold.

"How can you stand it down here?" exclaimed Dougal when he reached their bunk.

"Believe me, it's going to get much, much worse," said Mam. "A lot of folk have been seasick already and it's not even rough. Hold the baby for me. I need to straighten myself up." Dougal held his wet, screaming, red-faced baby sister at arm's length and tried to jiggle her out of her crying.

Flora and Maggie jumped down beside him.

"I was sick in the bucket last night," said Maggie in a small voice.

"I wasn't," boasted Flora.

Mam climbed down the bunk ladder and took back Wee Mary. "Empty the slop bucket, Dougal. I'll get our rations and we'll have breakfast up on deck." She shook her head. "What has your Da gotten us into?"

Dougal wanted to get back on deck as quickly as possible but so did the other settlers, and he had to wait his turn up the ladder. Everyone had their slop buckets and some folk were much better than others at getting to the top without splashing the contents. At least Dougal now knew which side of the ship to throw it over.

"That's better," said Mam when she and the girls joined him on deck a little while later. She tucked the straggles of her normally tidy hair behind her ears and breathed deeply. "Smell that fresh salty air." Dry and fed, Wee Mary was now soundly asleep in Mam's sling.

"Are we there yet?" whimpered Maggie, trying to look over the side without letting go of Mam's skirt or dropping Dolly.

"We've got a long way to go, pet. Let's sit down over here." They made themselves comfortable out of the wind, and Mam passed round the oatcakes she'd collected from the Bosun.

Flora took a bite, screwed up her face, spat out the mouthful, then vigorously wiped her tongue on the back of her hand. "Blaghhhh." She threw away the oatcake. Maggie copied her.

Dougal took a bite of his rock-hard disc. It had burnt edges and each mouthful took a lot of chewing and sucking before he could swallow it, but he was so hungry, he'd eat anything.

"Have some water," said Mam.

"The water tastes funny too," said Flora, spitting out the mouthful she'd just taken.

"You'll be hungry and thirsty later, my girl," warned Mam. "Now, we need to get into a routine, like at home. We'll all have chores to do every morning. The bucket must be emptied. The bedding shaken out. There will be laundry to do."

Dougal's attention drifted away. His eyes skittered around the ship. It was all so new and exciting. He didn't know what to look at first. He grinned to himself. At home he'd have been hard at work in the fields by now.

Smiley and another sailor caught his attention. They were chanting as they heaved on a rope. He turned and watched the boys who'd been skipping rocks at Loch Broom chase each other round the two big masts. Other kids were climbing on the gunwale and jumping down. He ached to join in.

"Dougal, are you listening?"

"Yes, Mam," said Dougal quickly.

"I was just saying, we must find our sea chest. It came aboard with the stores. Heaven knows where they've put it."

"I'll go and find it," said Dougal, jumping to his feet. "Right now."

"Away wi' you then."

Where to look first? Nearly all the settlers were up on deck, which made it really crowded, but who'd want to stay below any longer than they had to? Dougal squeezed his way round the edge of the ship, stopping every now and again to look over the side. All he could see was ocean and sky. There was no sign of land or another ship or even a bird.

Old Hugh and Janet walked by.

"Will you look at that," exclaimed Hugh, stooping to pick up a half eaten oatcake. He put it in his canvas bag. "This is no time to be wasting food."

"Get away wi' you, you old miser," Janet scolded. "You're an embarrassment, so you are."

In spite of the overcrowded deck, the tag game was growing like a hungry sea monster. Dougal itched to join in but he was on a mission. Shrieking and squealing, the children swirled between the passengers and jumped over the blocks and shackles, knocking over the neatly coiled ropes.

"Watch out! Flippin' kids!" Cursing loudly, an old sailor shook his fists at the sea monster then recoiled the tangled ropes.

"The ship's swarming with the brats," said another seaman. "Heard Cap'n say there's over seventy on-board. Seventy! I'd lock 'em all in the hold if it was up to me. Let 'em out when we get there."

"Or put 'em to work," said the old sailor. "Give me bones a rest."

Suddenly a tall lad crashed into Dougal, spinning him round and knocking him to the floor. Dougal stayed where he was until what seemed like every kid on the ship had either jumped on or over him.

"You all right?" said Smiley, yanking Dougal up onto his feet. "Get after them. It was that big fella knocked you down. The one with the carroty hair. Give him a punch and then another one from me." Smiley balled his fists in a demonstration.

"Another time," laughed Dougal. "I've got to find our sea chest, then I plan on exploring the ship."

Smiley snorted. "Explore! You'd see it all from here if folk'd get out the way."

"I suppose," said Dougal, not convinced there weren't lots of nooks and crannies to poke about in.

"Hey! I just remembered. There's a pile of boxes and gear waiting to be stowed outside the Captain's cabin. Try there."

"Thanks," said Dougal.

Smiley skipped off and Dougal made his way, through the crowds holidaying in the sunshine, to the back of the ship. The Captain came out of his cabin. "I've seen barnacles move faster than this, Bosun. There's a good stiff breeze. Put up every inch of sail we've got."

"Aye, aye, sir." The Bosun then bellowed a string of words so tangled together that Dougal had no idea what he was saying. Smiley understood though and, barefooted with two other sailors, he scrambled up the ratlines and balanced along the cross spars. They were so high that Dougal had to shade his eyes to watch them. He wished he was up there too. The patched topsails dropped into place, the deck tilted, and the *Hector* picked up speed.

"Don't you think sails are amazing?" said Dougal as Smiley swung himself back onto the deck. "They're just pieces of cloth but they can catch the wind and pull a ship right across the ocean."

"What the heck you on about?" Shaking his head, Smiley looped the rope he was holding over a peg then joined two other crew members turning the capstan to pull in the sails.

Dougal started searching through the stack of boxes and crates at his feet, shifting the top ones about so he could see the ones underneath.

"Get away from there!"

Dougal looked up as the shadow of the Bosun fell over him.

"Catch you messing with this stuff again, you'll know all about it." The Bosun pulled aside his jacket so the leather strap tied round his ample belly was plainly visible.

"I was just looking for…" mumbled Dougal, then decided to run rather than explain about their missing sea chest.

He dashed in and out of the settlers milling about the deck and didn't stop until he reached the back of the ship, where Smiley was swabbing the deck.

"Find it?" asked Smiley.

"No, the Bosun chased me off."

"Better move fast when he's after you," warned Smiley with a knowing wink. "I've nearly finished here. I can keep watch if you want to go back for another look?"

"Nah, I know it's not there. Da and I made it. I'd recognize even the smallest corner."

"It'll be down below then."

"That's what I was thinking," said Dougal, grimacing at the thought of searching the *Hector*'s miserable hold. "Where you from, Smiley? Where's your home?" he asked, putting off the moment.

"Liverpool. But my folks passed away long ago. This ship's my home." He stamped the deck with his foot. "If not this ship then another. I'm not fussy."

Dougal was about to say how awful it must be not having a home when he realized that this ship was the only home he had at the moment. But he did still have a family—well, except for a Da.

On his way to the hatch, Dougal saw Johnny Piper leaning over the side of the ship.

"How about a tune, piper?" said a settler.

Johnny Piper retched.

Jacqueline Halsey

The man laughed. "Later then."

Johnny Piper moaned, slumping down onto the deck. He opened one eye and spotted Dougal. "Coming on this voyage was a big mistake. I should've stayed home." His tanned face had turned the same dingy grey colour as the sails.

"Mam packed some herbs in our sea chest," said Dougal. "She'll have something to make you better. I've just got to find it."

"It's at the back of the hold on the right hand side."

"How do you know that?"

"I put it there. It's the one I helped bring on-board."

"I'll be right back," said Dougal.

CHAPTER 9

AFTER THE BRIGHT SUNLIGHT, IT TOOK A moment for Dougal's eyes to adjust to the darkness of the hold. The strained groans of the old hull sounded louder and more worrisome down here. The few settlers dotted below were either organizing their belongings or moaning with seasick groans behind their curtained-off bunks.

Dougal found the sea chest exactly where Johnny said it would it be, and dragged it to the deserted front section of the ship. He was almost at Mam's bunk when he heard raised voices. They were coming from the other side of an old piece of canvas that had been strung up to separate the settlers' quarters from the bow area.

Dougal peeked round the canvas wall and saw the carpenter and the Bosun squatting in front of a darker looking section of the hull. Dougal could see dribbles of water glistening in the glow of the oil lamp. A rat scooted by, but neither of the men seemed to notice.

"Fix the blinkin' leak!" The Bosun's bushy eyebrows met in a fierce line over his eyes. "It's what you're paid for, man."

"Can't perform miracles," snapped the carpenter. He poked at the wood around the crack. A wad of wet chips fell away in his hands. "See! This is what I was telling you about. Feel it fer yerself, it's soft as butter."

"Knew I shouldn't have signed up for this trip," swore the Boson, choosing not to touch the sodden wood.

The carpenter leaned back on his heels and rubbed his stubbly chin. "All ships leak, 'course they do. Usually I wedges in some tarry oakum straw and that does the trick, but look here." He pushed his fingers into the wood, circling further and further away from the leak. "It's all spongy. This is a big area, there's nothing hard for the oakum to grip on to."

"How much of the hull is rotten?" asked the Bosun.

"Dunno," said the carpenter. "If it's rotten here, you can bet yer life it'll be rotten someplace else."

Dougal couldn't believe what he was hearing. They hadn't even been at sea for twenty-four hours yet. If the whole hull was like this bit, they'd be at the bottom of the ocean before they were halfway across. Smiley's knotty rope wasn't going to save them from filling up with water and sinking.

"You gonna get the Captain?" asked the carpenter.

"Nah! Captain's got one heck of a temper and I'd be the one on the end of it. I'll wait to see if any more leaks appear before I tell him. Never know, it might just be this one spot."

"Keep dreaming," said the carpenter, under his breath.

"Tell me right off if you find others. You hear?"

"Don't you worry, you'll be the first to hear about any leaks I find."

"Right," said the Bosun.

"And I'll tar some canvas over this rotten stuff," said the carpenter. "Haven't got enough to go over the whole frikkin' ship though." He laughed in a humourless way.

"What's that?" The Bosun jerked his head in Dougal's direction.

"Didn't hear anything."

Dougal quickly let the canvas fall, and shrank back into the shadows.

"Keep your voice down," hissed the Bosun. "I think someone's there. If this gets out we'll have a riot on our hands."

"Don't worry. Most only speaks that funny gobble-dygarlic language. They won't know what we're talking about."

But Dougal could speak English. He *did* know what they were talking about.

"I'll get my tools," said the carpenter.

"And I'll get the boy started on the chain pump. We'll keep it going round the clock if need be."

The two men came back through the curtain. Dougal stayed as still as a statue, not daring to breathe until both sets of boots had disappeared up the ladder.

So Old Hugh was right, he thought. The ship was rotten, and they were somewhere in the middle of the ocean and would probably sink at any minute. Dougal's heart was racing. This was a terrible discovery. He tapped the nearest piece of hull with his knuckles just like the carpenter had. It seemed sound enough. Then he climbed up to Mam's bunk and tapped along that part of the hull. That seemed okay too, but what did he know about leaking hulls? Should he tell Mam or the Captain or anybody?

When he came back on deck, Mam was standing over a small sandbox fireplace. Isobel stood next to her, stroking her round belly. Janet was there too with a couple of other women Dougal hadn't seen before. They were laughing as they struggled to cook and keep their balance on the swaying deck. A bunch of little kids bopped around their legs.

"I found our sea chest," said Dougal.

"Good," said Mam, smiling over at him. "Don't need it at the moment but I surely will. What's the matter, Dougal? You look pale. Are you getting sick?" Mam left her stirring and felt Dougal's face. "I want to know if you feel the slightest bit ill, you understand?"

"I'm fine," said Dougal. He brushed Mam's hand away and fixed a smile on his face, but it was hard to keep it there with visions of the rotting hull hanging like a black cloud over his head.

"Good," said Mam.

"But Johnny Piper's really seasick." He'd almost forgotten about the piper.

"I'm sure it will pass, but I'll go and check on him."

"Mam," said Dougal.

"Yes?"

"Never mind." Dougal sat down beside Maggie who was playing with Wee Mary. He knew his Da wouldn't have worried his Mam with a problem they could do nothing about. He decided that if the Bosun wasn't telling the Captain, he wouldn't tell Mam. But he was going to keep close to the carpenter. He was one who knew about these things.

By the time Mam was back from seeing to Johnny Piper, dinner was ready. Flora, with her arms stretched wide, followed by her new arm-flapping friends, swooped over and sat down. "We're seagulls," she said.

Dougal rolled his eyes. The women ladled out the soup.

When he'd finished his meal, Dougal put his hands behind his back and tapped the hull to see if this part was spongy. Maggie saw him and started tapping too. *Uh oh*, thought Dougal. He couldn't let her find out what he was up to. He quickly tapped some more, making out it was a game.

"You two got some music going?" said Johnny Piper, beating a rhythm with his feet on the deck as he came up to them.

"Feeling better?" asked Dougal.

"Your Mam's amazing. She said I should eat an oatcake and fix my eyes on the horizon. It worked." He sat down, picked up Mam's wooden spoon, and started drumming.

Dougal caught the beat and joined in, while Maggie bashed away on anything she could find.

"Let's join the ceilidh," cried Flora. The 'seagulls' clapped and banged along too. Finally Johnny did a great drum roll on the upturned hull of the longboat, then held up his hands and the band stopped.

There were cheers. They had an audience. "Piper, play us a tune," called someone from the crowd.

Johnny Piper's face lit into a huge smile. He handed Dougal the wooden spoon, hustled off, and returned with his bagpipes. "Dougal, play the rhythm I showed you."

Dougal drummed.

"Great," said Johnny. "Keep it up, louder on the first beat. That's it." He blew into the bag and started playing.

As Dougal drummed he listened to the pipes. He loved the quick notes that joined the rich chords and the throaty background sounds. He'd been too busy standing guard to really notice them at Loch Broom.

The deck was transformed into a party. There was dancing and hooting and clapping just like on the beach the night before they left.

Johnny Piper collapsed in a happy, breathless heap on the blanket. "Can't play anymore," he said. The settlers patted him on the back and dispersed. As he stowed away his bagpipes, he turned to Dougal. "You've got a good sense of rhythm."

"Really?"

"Yes." He studied Dougal's face for a long moment. "I could teach you to play the bagpipes. That is, if you want to learn."

"If I want to learn?" Dougal's mouth gaped open and he stared unbelievingly at Johnny Piper. In his head were the faces of the villagers back home watching him standing on the deck, the forbidden instrument splayed out over his shoulders. *Wee Dougie Cameron playing the bagpipes. Fancy that,* they would say. And Da's face would glow with pride and Ruari would be so jealous. Of course, neither his Da nor anyone in the village would ever see or hear him play, but the people in New Scotland would. He'd be a piper.

"You'd really teach me how to play the bagpipes?"

"We'll start right now," said Johnny Piper, standing up. "Follow me to Piper Corner."

CHAPTER 10

PIPER CORNER WAS JOHNNY PIPER'S HOME behind the water barrels. He had just enough room to lie down beside his pipes. Dougal squeezed after him into the narrow space and watched as Piper took the bagpipes apart. Naming each piece, he laid them on the blanket one by one. "Tenor drone, great drone, chanter, bag, blowpipe, chords." Then he carefully tied them up.

Dougal's face dropped. "Oh! I thought you were going to teach me how to play today."

"I am," said Piper. He patted his beloved bagpipes snug in their blanket. "This is a very difficult instrument to play and I'm going to teach you exactly the way my grandfather taught me. I've never taught anyone to play before and I want to do it right." He pulled out a long reed pipe and handed it to Dougal. "This is a practice chanter. You have to learn to play this first."

Dougal put the pipe in his mouth and blew as hard as he could.

Jacqueline Halsey

"Stop" cried Johnny Piper. "Not like that." He took a deep breath. "Watch me. You have to hold the pipe lightly. Thumbs at the back, fingers straight, wrists straight, elbows out."

Dougal grimaced. "All at the same time?"

Piper positioned Dougal's arms and fingers. "Now cover the holes one by one starting at the bottom—good—now blow steadily."

Dougal blew. It didn't sound quite right.

"Again," said Johnny Piper.

Dougal tried again…and again…and again. At last he got a good note. He grinned from ear to ear. "I did it."

"Well done, Dougal. But enough for today, lesson two tomorrow." Johnny Piper smiled and patted Dougal on the shoulder. "I'm so happy to be teaching you and fulfilling Grandfather's promise, I really am." He smiled. "I just never realized how much patience my grandfather had," he added under his breath.

～～

Every afternoon, Dougal went for his bagpipe lesson. As soon as Dougal could play a scale, Johnny Piper let him keep the chanter to practice.

Dougal practiced a lot. He only put the chanter down to eat, sleep, do whatever chores Mam needed doing, and cut his daily notches on the gunwale. There were now seventeen of them. He wasn't interested in watching the on-deck wrestling matches, or listening to Old Hugh's tall stories. He didn't even join in the obstacle races up, over, and under anything and everything on the deck, even though he knew he could out-race any kid on-board.

Smiley gave up on trying to get Dougal to hang out with him when he wasn't on watch. Dougal's intention to follow the carpenter around hadn't happened either. Games and rotting hulls weren't nearly as important as learning to play the bagpipes.

One by one the squeaks and wrong notes disappeared. Playing the chanter began to feel easy and Dougal wondered how he'd ever found it hard.

At the very first lesson, Johnny Piper had said he'd only attach the bag to the pipe when Dougal could play a scale on the chanter smoothly without stumbling. One step at a time. That's how his grandfather had taught him.

Dougal leaned back against the side of the hull with a satisfied look on his face. Today was the day he'd show Johnny Piper he was ready for the next step. He put the chanter in his mouth again, placed his fingers firmly over the holes, and blew steadily down the mouthpiece.

"Make him stop!" cried Flora, clapping her hands over her ears.

"Please," said Mam.

Dougal glared at his sister. She had a triumphant look in her green eyes. Reluctantly, he laid down the chanter.

With a wicked grin, Flora picked it up and ran off.

"Get back here," yelled Dougal, but before he could get to his feet, one of the bigger kids had snatched the pipe off her. Dougal leapt after him. "No!" He was about to grab it, when the pipe got passed to another kid, who snuck it behind his back to a girl who waved it in the air before throwing it to someone else. To shouts of "piggy-in-the-middle" and shrieks of laughter, Dougal became the best game on deck. He didn't care about the teasing, he just wanted the precious chanter back.

"Come and get it," a boy sang out. As Dougal lunged, the boy tossed the chanter high into the air. Dougal watched the pipe spin over his head to the other side of the ship.

This can't be happening, thought Dougal. Johnny Piper had told him how his grandfather had made him the practice chanter from a hollow reed and together they'd burned in the holes with a red-hot rod. He could never ever face him again if the pipe got damaged—or worse, thrown overboard. He stopped and leaned back on a barrel, faking that he couldn't care less about the pipe.

They'll soon get bored, he thought, *especially if I stop playing their stupid game*. All the faces blurred together as Dougal focused on keeping the chanter in sight. But when the chanter whizzed past his nose, he couldn't help himself. He dove for the pipe, missed, and tripped over Old Hugh, who was picking up scraps off the deck.

"Watch yerself, laddie!"

Dougal struggled to his feet. "Where's the chanter?" he cried, to no one in particular.

"Saw one of them go down into the hold," said a settler. "Couldn't see if he had your pipe or not."

Dougal raced over to the hatch. *Bet they jump me*, he thought as he clattered down the ladder, but he didn't care. He had to get the chanter back.

There was no sign of them. *Must be hiding*. Dougal listened. The only sounds were the usual creaks and groans of the old hull, the pounding of feet on the deck above, the slosh of water, and the thump of the chain pump. He slowly moved up and down the aisles looking all about him as he went. If only there was more light. The few dim oil lamps just made the shadows darker.

"You've had your fun, now give me back the pipe," he called out, trying to sound forceful. That never worked on Flora or the kids back home, so why he thought anyone here would listen to him, he didn't know. "We could use my Mam's big wooden spoon for the game," he added. That was a total lie. Mam would never let that spoon out of her sight.

There was no answer. No shuffling, giggling, or whispering, just the muffled moans of seasick folk behind their curtains. *They've hidden it and gone back on deck*, thought Dougal as he looked about in despair. Lines of washing drooped between the curtained-off bunks, creating dark, gloomy spaces. The chanter could be anywhere.

Suddenly, a hand slid out of the bunk in front of him and hung there white and shiny and still. Dougal startled. His first thought was to race back on deck, but something made him reach out and touch it. The clammy hand grasped his fingers. He lifted a corner of the curtain. Lying side by side were a woman and a girl. They were both shivering and their faces glistened with sweat.

The woman raised her head. "Need water." Her dry voice hardly made it over her cracked lips. "For my Lass," she said, sinking back in exhaustion.

"I'll get help," said Dougal, and ran back on the deck, shouting all the way. "Mam! Mam!"

"Dougal, slow down," said Mam, as he came panting up to the longboat. "Flora has something to say to you."

"Mam. This is important."

"Listen to your sister first."

"I'm sorry I took your pipe, I mean chanter," said Flora, and flung her arms around him. Dougal stood there stiffly and didn't attempt to hug her back. He didn't think she was one bit sorry, and so what if she was, 'sorry' wouldn't bring back the chanter. It was gone and with it his dream of being a piper. Johnny would never teach him now.

He broke free of Flora and turned back to Mam.

"There's a woman and a girl down there. They're sick with fever. I've got to get them some water."

Mam's smile slipped from her face before Dougal finished talking. She rapidly untied Wee Mary from her shawl and gave the baby to Dougal. "Stay on deck with the girls. Don't let them below under any circumstances." With that, she picked up what was left of their day's water ration and disappeared into the hold.

Half an hour later Mam came back on deck, her mouth set in a thin tight line. She marched past Dougal straight up to the Captain, who was standing with his hands behind his back, smiling smugly up at the stiff breeze filling the sails.

Dougal caught up with his mother. "What is it, Mam?"

"Good day to you," said the Captain with a formal nod.

"It is not a good day at all, Captain Spiers," said Mam. "Far from it."

"More complaints, I fear," he replied, still smiling.

"Sir, I have grave news to report. There are two cases of smallpox on-board."

The Captain's smile changed to an expression of horror as her words sunk in. "Surely it's just seasickness, or a chill from the damp air."

Mam pulled Dougal round in front of her. He could feel her hands trembling under his chin as she tilted his head up towards the Captain. "Look at my son's face. These are pox scars. I lost two sons to this dreadful disease. Sir, I know smallpox when I see it."

Dougal pulled away. "Sorry, son," whispered Mam. She knew he hated any attention drawn to his bumpy face.

Dougal couldn't remember being ill. He'd been only five, the same age Maggie was now. His two little brothers had been sick too. He got better. They didn't. Sometimes he'd lie in bed and try to remember what they looked like, but their faces never quite came to him.

"And this is the smallpox," Mam was saying. "We must isolate the affected pair immediately or it will spread throughout the ship."

"Tell me, ma'am," said the Captain. "Where in this God-forsaken, overcrowded ship could we possibly isolate anybody?"

CHAPTER 11

"HUSH, HUSH, WEE MARY. MAM WILL BE BACK soon," said Dougal for the hundredth time. He shifted the baby onto his other hip and moved nearer the hatchway, hoping Mam would hear her screaming and come up the ladder. He jumped back as a horrific thought came into his head. Supposing the smallpox germs were rising from the hold like an invisible cloud of mosquitoes and falling all over Wee Mary's pretty face.

Dougal paced some more, bouncing his little sister higher with each step. Then he lifted her over his head and twirled her around. This used to make her giggle, but not today. Dougal spotted Johnny Piper through the crowd and veered quickly off to the right so as not to bump into him and have to explain about the chanter. This manoeuver brought him face to face with the Loch Broom stone throwers.

"Ahhh! Doesn't he make a lovely Mammy?" said one.

"Wish I had a Mammy like him," said another. They swaggered into each other, snorting with laughter as they walked away.

Dougal pretended to ignore them. But they'd made him feel pretty stupid. Looking after a baby was woman's work.

"Why is Mam staying in the hold so long, Wee Mary? She's been down there ever since she told the Captain about the smallpox and that was a very long time ago."

His baby sister answered with a renewed, louder-than-ever bout of screaming. How could anyone that small make so much noise? Her open mouth seemed to take up her whole face, which was now as red as a beetroot. Dougal tried giving her his finger to suck like Mam sometimes did, but she wouldn't take it. His finger probably smelled bad. He wouldn't want to put it in his own mouth. He went back to their corner.

"Shh, Wee Mary, I've just put Dolly to sleep," said Maggie.

The baby took no notice.

"Here, let me have her," said Janet. "Goodness me, the poor wee bairn's soaked through. We'll use my kerchief for a napkin and see if that will soothe her." Janet sang while she changed the baby and Wee Mary stopped crying, but as soon as she was back in Dougal's arms she started up again. Dougal pointed out the main mast and the mizzen mast and the jib sail. He'd learned quite a lot about ships since he'd been on-board, but Wee Mary just wanted Mam to nurse her.

The day was ending and a light rain misted over the *Hector*. At long last Mam came back on deck. She was laden with their quilts and shawls. After dropping them on their patch of deck, she flopped down and held out her arms for Wee Mary. It was suddenly peaceful.

"We're all sleeping up here tonight," she declared.

"I'm cold," said Maggie.

"It's raining," said Flora. "We'll get wet."

"I know," said Mam, "but it's healthier up here. We'll snuggle up together. That'll keep us warm."

Johnny Piper came over. Dougal shuffled his feet and stared hard at the deck.

"Judging by all the quilts, it looks like you're joining the deck sleepers tonight," he said brightly. Then his smile vanished. "You wouldn't be doing that if the rumour about there being smallpox aboard wasn't true."

"Two people are very sick indeed," said Mam. "They must have already had the disease when they came onboard." Her expression was grim. "Now it's here, it will stay. There will be tears, and lots of them."

"How are the patients, Mrs. Cameron?" said Captain Spiers, joining them. "Oh! I apologize for my intrusion." He looked away.

Mam quickly pulled her shawl over the baby's head to cover herself up. "Not good, but they're holding their own."

"Glad to hear it. Any more cases?"

"Not yet, sir."

"Good, good." The Captain rocked on his heels and looked up at the sails sagging from the spars. "We'll not be going far tonight," he muttered. "More's the pity." Then with head down and hands clasped behind his back, he strode away.

The mist turned into a heavy drizzle and the deck became deserted as, one by one, the settlers scuttled below out of the rain. Flora and Maggie tried, unsuccessfully, to drape a quilt over all their heads to keep them dry.

"Dougal, are you thinking what I'm thinking?" said Johnny Piper.

Dougal doubted that, seeing as how he was still thinking how to tell Johnny Piper he'd lost his chanter. He hadn't realized he'd been staring at the upturned longboat.

"The longboat," exclaimed Dougal. "It looks like a roof. It'll make a great shelter."

"Exactly," said Johnny. "Help me wedge that box under one side so the gap's big enough to crawl under."

"Quick, girls," said Mam. "In out of the rain."

Flora and Maggie scrambled under the boat, pulling the quilts after them. "Here's the chanter," shrieked Flora, waving the pipe in the air.

"What!" Dougal snatched it out of her hand. "You had it all the time?"

"Did not. I found it poked under the side here."

It was too dim to see the expression on Flora's face but Dougal didn't believe her for one minute. He turned to Johnny Piper and handed over the chanter. "I sort of misplaced it this morning."

"No matter, it's found now," said Johnny Piper. He placed his fingers on the pipe, and as everyone hunkered down for the night, he started to play. It was a haunting tune, familiar and yet not. It sounded like lochs and heather and ancient mountains.

Dougal lay in the darkness listening to the notes as they mixed with his sisters' sleepful breathing, the slap of the waves and the rain drumming on their

longboat roof. He wanted to remember every note and he wanted this to be the very first song he'd play on the bagpipes—that is, if Johnny ever trusted him with any part of the precious instrument again.

~~

Dougal was the first to crawl out from under the longboat the next morning. It had stopped raining but there was still no wind. The old ship slumped up and down with the waves in no hurry to go anywhere.

After peeing, and carving the day's notch, Dougal went back to the longboat and discovered that Mam's cookpot had caught an inch or so of rain. There was enough for each of them to have one big gulp of fresh water. It was more delicious than anything he'd ever tasted.

As they were finishing breakfast, Smiley raced up. "We're fishing off the stern. Look lively, I've only got an hour before my next shift at the chain pump."

Dougal hooted, scrambling to his feet.

Mam put a hand on his arm. "Sorry, Dougal, I need you to look after the baby. I've got to tend my patients. If I'm right, the spots will appear today. It's a dangerous time, although I must admit some fish would be a welcome change from all the salt beef we've been having."

A look of sheer disbelief spread over Dougal's face. How could Mam possibly think of not letting him go fishing?

"Can Flora and Maggie look after her?" said Dougal. "Maggie's much better with Wee Mary than me anyway."

Mam folded her arms across her chest and Dougal knew by the expression on her face that he was not going fishing today.

"They can help," she said, "but I need you in charge."

He looked at his baby sister cooing on the blanket. She was happy now, but after her nap she'd be screaming for her Mammy just like yesterday. The thought of spending another day walking the deck, jiggling Wee Mary, when he could be fishing was unbearable.

"Too bad," said Smiley. "But I'll bring you a fish so at least you'll still get your fish dinner." He turned and crashed into Janet who was walking by with Old Hugh.

"Watch it, laddie," shouted Old Hugh, putting his hand out to steady his wife. "Young whippersnapper!"

"Sorry," called Smiley and raced off.

"Are you all right?" asked Mam.

"No harm done," said Janet, straightening her dress. "I couldn't help overhearing. You know, I could watch the baby and Dougal could catch some fish for us too."

"Really?" Dougal looked pleadingly at his Mam. "I won't be gone all day. Just an hour, maybe two."

"Go on then," she said.

"Thanks Mam, thanks Janet. Tonight we'll all have the best fish dinner ever. You wait and see."

"Hrrrph," said Old Hugh, stroking his chin. "Done quite a bit of fishing in my time. I think I'd best come and show you how to do it."

Dougal was about to make a face, but decided to hide the fact that he'd rather be fishing with Smiley than with grouchy Old Hugh in case Mam changed her mind. After all, fishing with anyone was a whole lot better than babysitting.

Janet laughed. "He might be sixty years old, but my Hugh's still a wee laddie on the inside."

Dougal jogged after Old Hugh, who had walked off in the wrong direction. Hugh's head was down and Dougal had no idea what the old man was looking for. *Better not be mouldy oatcakes*, he thought.

"Ah ha," cried Hugh, at last. He bent down and picked something up. In Old Hugh's gnarly outspread hand was a bent nail. He showed it to Dougal. "See if you can find us a couple more like this."

"A fish hook! Brilliant!" Dougal searched between the barrels and crates and soon they'd found six more between them.

"Now we need some bait." Old Hugh hobbled over to the hatch.

Dougal stayed where he was. "I'm not allowed down there."

"'Cos of the smallpox?"

Dougal nodded. Hugh turned back and put his hands on Dougal's shoulders.

"Young fella, I've got more pox scars than stars in the sky. They're hidden under my whiskers. Now seeing how there's no getting the smallpox twice, by my reckoning you and me are both safe to go below."

Dougal squinted into Old Hugh's face. It was tanned and blotchy but, looking closely between the wrinkles, Dougal recognized the dent of a pox scar, high on Hugh's cheekbone. There were a couple more on his forehead. How come he hadn't noticed them before?

Dougal touched his own face and for the first time ever, he didn't mind the feel of his pitted cheeks. He was nearly thirteen. His whiskers would be sprouting soon and when they did, he'd grow himself the biggest, fluffiest beard in the whole of Scotland. Well, New Scotland. His pox scars would be gone from sight forever.

Dougal followed Old Hugh down the ladder, into the hold. He held his nose against the overpowering stench. It was much worse than the last time he'd been below. When they reached Old Hugh's bunk, the old man pulled aside the curtain. Even in the poor light, Dougal could see the splintering planks on the far wall. Old Hugh leaned over and picked some grubs out of the rotting wood with his fingers. "Ha," he said. "Now we have our bait."

Dougal was stunned. "It's rotted right through up in the bow, you know," he blurted out. "Water's actually coming in. I saw it. They've got the chain pumps working all the time. The Bosun's worried but he won't tell the Captain in case he gets into trouble. The water may come through here too."

Dougal expected Old Hugh to charge over to the Captain, roaring and ranting as he went, but the old man just kept picking grubs out of the blackened wood. He put some in the tin and some in his mouth.

"*Uch!*" said Dougal. "Did you hear what I said about the leak?"

"Aye, laddie, I did. I knew she was rotten the minute I clapped eyes on her." He sounded almost smug that he'd been proven right. "Grubs are good protein by the way."

"I'm not eating them," said Dougal, screwing up his face in disgust. "Are we going to sink in the middle of the ocean?"

"It's in God's hands, laddie," said Old Hugh. "Now stop your blathering, we've got dinner to catch."

"Dougal Angus Cameron. What are you doing down here?"

Dougal turned towards the shout. The look on Mam's face was scarier than the dripping hull. He hid his hand containing the grubs behind his back. "Hugh, umm, wanted to get something. It's okay, we've both had small-pox—you can't get it twice."

"Get yourself up on deck this minute and don't you dare let me see you down here again."

"Yes, Mam. I mean no, Mam," said Dougal, dodging round his mother and scooting up the ladder as fast as he possibly could.

CHAPTER 12

HANDLINING FOR COD WITH OLD HUGH, Smiley, and Johnny Piper was the very best part of the voyage so far. Dougal had never seen such big fish and they sure did love the grubs. There was enough fish for everybody who wanted some, including the crew. Janet looked after Wee Mary and took over the cooking while Mam looked after her patients. For two days there were huge helpings of baked fish for lunch and fish soup for supper.

"Janet's a better cook than Mam," whispered Flora, licking out her bowl on the second evening.

"Is not," said Maggie.

Dougal kind of agreed with Flora. He licked his lips and scraped every last morsel from his bowl. He didn't say anything though.

On the third morning the wind picked up, the sails filled, the deck slanted, and the *Hector* was on her way again.

"Move," yelled the Bosun. "Can't get the sails up if we're tripping over you blinking kids." Dougal dodged out of the way and watched the crew scramble into action. High in the rigging and down on the deck, they heaved and tugged the sails into place to catch the wind.

Dougal leaned over the side. A frothy wake rolled away from the *Hector*'s bows. The sunlight shone through the churning water, making it look bright turquoise one moment and darkest blue the next.

"Unfortunately, laddie, fish cannae swim this fast," said Old Hugh. A rare chuckle squeezed through his bristly whiskers. Dougal felt his own chin just in case a whisker had appeared overnight. After all, that's when Da's whiskers grew.

"No fishing today then," said Dougal.

"There'll be other days." Old Hugh shuffled off with his canvas bag, stooping as he went to add more discarded oatcakes to his collection.

Dougal knew he should be getting back to Mam, but he loved the tarry, salty smell of the ocean and how it was always changing. He'd just finished carving notch number twenty on the gunwale when Johnny Piper came up. "It surely is a bright, beautiful morning," he said.

"Aye! No fishing though."

"A music morning then," said Piper.

"You mean another bagpipe lesson? I didn't lose the chanter you know. Flora—"

"Och! Never mind about that."

"And I can play the scales without stopping," said Dougal.

"Then I'll show you how the pipes fit onto the bag."

Dougal jumped up in the air, then his face dropped. "I'll have to check with Mam. She spends most of her time in the hold looking after the smallpox patients, especially now that other people are getting sick. Janet might not want to spend another day looking after our baby if I can't pay her with a fish." Dougal made a face. "Oh, and I've got chores as well."

"I'll meet you at Piper Corner when you're free. Good job we're out of sight behind those water barrels. The minute folk see me take out the pipes they expect a concert."

"I'll be there as soon as I can," said Dougal and made his way back to the longboat.

"There's no fishing today," he said as he hurried through the morning chores. "So would it be all right if—"

"Could you draw up a bucket of sea water? I need to do some laundry," said Mam, gathering together the dirty clothes.

Dougal drew up the water. "Mam, could I—"

"Thanks, Dougal. Honestly one pint of water each a day for everything. It's ridiculous. That's not even enough for drinking and cooking let alone keeping ourselves clean. Still it's a good day to do the laundry even if it is in salt water. The sun and this stiff breeze will have everything dry in no time."

"You see, Johnny Piper said he'd give me—"

"Help Flora with the bedding for me," interrupted Mam for a third time.

Flora dragged out a quilt and Dougal took two corners and helped her shake it. Before they'd finished spreading it out to air, her dancing seagulls came by. Flora skipped off to join them.

"Flora, come back," said Dougal. "We're not done yet."

Mam laughed. "Away to your bagpipes. Maggie and I can finish up here. I'll check on my patients after your lesson."

"Thanks, Mam." Dougal ran off, then came back to give her a quick kiss before heading to Johnny Piper's hideaway behind the barrels.

Johnny was sitting cross-legged with the bagpipes laid out in bits in front of him. The deck rolled and Dougal lurched. "Sit," said Johnny. "Now hold this for me."

Dougal's insides bubbled with excitement as he took the bag part of the bagpipe from Johnny. This would be the start of real piping. He ran his hands over the old hide bag, smoothed shiny by the years. It had been patched many times and he wondered who'd sewn the tiny stitches round each patch.

"The blow pipe goes here," said Johnny, fitting a small pipe with a mouthpiece into the top of the bag. "And the chanter fits into the bottom. We'll add the drones later. They're for the background sound. Now, tuck the pipe in the side of your mouth and blow in short, rhythmic puffs to fill the bag."

Dougal took in a lungful of air and blew into the bag.

"Steady puffs," said Johnny. "Sort of like panting."

Very slowly, the bag plumped up. By the time Johnny said "That's enough," Dougal felt like he had a plucked chicken under his arm. His eyes felt like they were about to pop out of his head.

"You'll soon get the hang of breathing and blowing. Once the bag's full of air it's easier to keep her topped up."

"Phew," said Dougal. "Couldn't keep that up much longer. Blowing and breathing, something else to learn."

"Now we need to stand up. This might get interesting." With feet wide apart, Dougal tried to keep his balance as Johnny adjusted the bag under Dougal's left arm. He put the mouthpiece of the blow pipe back in Dougal's mouth and positioned his fingers on the chanter. "Now blow as you breathe, squeeze slowly as you blow, and let your fingers play the first notes of the scale."

Blow, breathe, squeeze, fingers. Blow, breathe, squeeze, fingers, Dougal repeated to himself. He took a lungful of air and blew. Nothing happened, then the bagpipe yowled. Dougal winced. Johnny laughed. "Don't blow so hard." Dougal nodded, and with his face scrunched tight with determination, tried again.

"Slow and steady," encouraged Johnny. "Feel the connection between your arm, your fingers, and your breathing—again—that's it—feel the rhythm—go on—let the bagpipes become part of you."

The bagpipe screeched as Dougal tried to get the blowing and pumping right. He rested then had another go. There was an occasional good note but mostly it sounded like he was sitting on a cat. "Enough for today," laughed Johnny. "You should have heard the noise I made at my first try. The crows put their wings over their ears."

"Crows don't have ears," said Dougal, smiling even though he felt desperately disappointed.

"Takes practice," said Johnny. "Wouldn't be special if it didn't."

"What was the tune you played that first night we sheltered from the rain under the longboat?"

"What, this one?" Johnny took back the bagpipes and played a few notes of the song.

Dougal nodded. "That's it." It sounded different with the bag and without the drumming rain but he still liked it, especially the little notes that joined up the chords. "What's it called?"

"Don't know. I made it up."

"I'm going to call it '*Hector*'s Rain Song,'" said Dougal. He took up the practice chanter and played the melody from memory.

"You've got a good ear," said Johnny. "We'll have another go tomorrow."

Day after day, as the old ship made her slow way across the Atlantic, Dougal disappeared into Piper Corner for his lesson. His head ached from blowing, his arms ached from pumping the bag, and his back ached from holding the heavy instrument, but he was determined to be a piper. Each time he inflated the bag he imagined himself playing wonderful, heart-stirring music, but when he started to play, his notes sounded more like cats fighting. Some days Dougal thought he'd never get it right but Johnny Piper said he was making progress.

One afternoon, about a week after they'd started their lessons, Dougal staggered across the bucking deck to the nook behind the barrels. He'd rushed through his chores, hoping to make his daily lesson a few minutes longer, but Johnny wasn't there, which was unusual. Dougal leaned back against the side and played an invisible set of bagpipes while he waited.

That morning he'd carved the twenty-seventh notch on the gunwale. It was nearly four weeks since they'd left Loch Broom. Mr. Ross had said the voyage would take four or five weeks. If that was true they were nearly there. Dougal frowned. Supposing there wasn't enough time to learn the bagpipes before they arrived or sank. The grim thought sort of slipped in but he pushed it aside. The possibility of not being able to play properly was the more likely. He'd have to try and get Johnny Piper to give him extra lessons.

Then another thought struck him—almost worse than sinking. If Johnny Piper didn't live close to them when they reached New Scotland, Dougal wouldn't have any bagpipes to play. He'd be a piper without pipes. Then again, why wouldn't Johnny Piper want to live near them, or even with them? They were his family now.

Johnny Piper arrived at last. "Sorry I'm late. I'm not feeling good today. Get the pipes ready, like I showed—" He clapped his hands over his mouth and raced back to the side.

Dougal assembled the bagpipes, inflated the bag, and waited.

Eventually, Johnny stumbled back. "Practice what we did yesterday," he said. "I'll sit here and listen. The waves are different today. Have you noticed? My stomach doesn't like them at all."

Dougal had noticed. The waves looked more like glassy rolling hills. The *Hector* would slide up a wave then rock to one side as it fell back down and rock to the other side as it righted itself. But Dougal wasn't interested in the waves. He wanted to start playing. He could manage a scale and the first few chords of the "*Hector*'s Rain song," with only an occasional cat yowl.

He took a large breath to fill his lungs. "Blow—squeeze—fingers," he said to himself, then he began playing. The deep rumbling chords filled their corner. He was finally getting the hang of it. Grey skies, bad water, burnt oatcakes, leaky ships, annoying sisters, wailing babies, his scarred face, Da dying, all these things disappeared. He really was starting to play the bagpipes. It also felt exciting and dangerous, even though there was no chance of getting arrested out in the middle of the ocean. He so wished his Da could hear him play.

"Stop a minute," said Johnny, standing up. "Something's happening on deck. Go and see what's going on." Dougal handed back the bagpipes and went and stood at the edge of the crowd that had formed round the Bosun. Standing on a crate, the Bosun held up his hand for quiet. His scowly face looked more creased than usual. *He's going to tell everyone about the leaking hull*, thought Dougal. *It must be getting worse.*

"Haven't got all day," bellowed the Bosun, "and I'm not going to keep repeating myself, so pass it on to any families not here." One of the settlers stood by his side and translated what he was saying into Gaelic.

Dougal could see Mam and Wee Mary at the front. He felt sick with apprehension. *I should have told Mam about the hull as soon as I found out*, he thought.

"The light winds mean we've lost a lot of time. To make the rations last, we'll be cutting food and water quotas, starting tomorrow. That's it. That's all I've got to say." The Bosun stepped down off the crate.

"I thought we were nearly there," said Dougal to the woman standing next to him.

"Me too," she replied, shaking her head.

"What do you mean, cut?" shouted out a man near the front.

"We don't have enough *now*," said Old Hugh, waving his fist in the air. "By how much? What about all the fish we caught? Explain yourself, man."

"I won't be saying any more," said the Bosun as he pushed his way through the crowd. "It isn't my fault, so don't go blaming. That's just how it is." He disappeared down below to a chorus of jeers and hisses.

Dougal joined in with the crowd, waving his arms and calling out. Janet came up and tapped him on the shoulder. "Get your Mam. She's needed urgently."

Dougal wriggled through the mass of angry bodies and fetched his mother.

"Did you hear all that?" said Mam, when she reached Janet. Her eyes were blazing. "As if conditions weren't bad enough. This is dreadful. We barely have enough water as it is and there's no milk for the children. I'm afraid my milk is waning. What I'll feed Wee Mary on when it—"

"It's worse, much worse" said Janet, interrupting Mam's tirade. "Two more children have come down with the smallpox."

"I knew there'd be more," said Mam, shaking her head. Her expression was grave.

"They're the sisters that play with your Flora," said Janet.

CHAPTER 13

THE COLOUR LEFT MAM'S FACE AS SHE PUSHED Wee Mary into Janet's open arms. "I'll go to them now," she said. But she couldn't move. Flora had flung her arms round Mam's legs and was sobbing hard into the folds of her skirts.

"Hush now, Flora, I'm going to look after your friends," said Mam.

"Am I…g…going…to get s…s…smallpox?" Flora asked through hiccupy sobs.

Mam bent down. "Look at me. I know you're scared, and I don't know whether or not you'll catch the smallpox, but if you do I'll take the best care of you I can. You know that, don't you?"

Flora nodded.

"You must let me go to your friends now, they need me."

Flora let go of Mam's skirts and with tears still streaming down her cheeks, she said, "I don't want to look like Dougal."

Dougal heard Mam suck in her breath as he turned away, blinking hard to stop the tears. *Only babies cry*, he told himself firmly. He wasn't a baby, he was the man of the family.

Mam put her hand on his shoulder. "She's only a little girl," she said, quietly. "Just a silly wee girl. She didn't mean to be hurtful." Dougal liked the feel of Mam's warm hand. He wanted it to stay, but Mam had to go. She hurried away, only stopping to call back, "On no circumstances are any of you to come down into the hold. You understand? No circumstances whatsoever. I'll be back to nurse Wee Mary in a little while."

Dougal wiped his nose on the back of his hand and scuffed along after Janet, Flora, and Maggie to their corner by the longboat. Janet sat down against the side of the ship and bounced Wee Mary on her lap.

"Pass around the water, Dougal, there's a dear," she said. "I'm parched and it must be lunchtime. You hand out the oatcakes, Flora." There was just one mouthful of water each, and even though it tasted like pond slime, Dougal could have drunk the whole pitcher. He took an oatcake from Flora but couldn't look at her. If his own sister thought he was that ugly, what did everyone else think?

He still had years and years of being ugly before his whiskers hid the scars. Da didn't have a beard maybe because he didn't have any scars to hide. Dougal remembered watching him shave his face every morning with a long sharp knife. He didn't know how long stubbly whiskers took to grow into a bushy beard. He sighed, sad that Da wasn't here anymore to answer questions like that.

Dark furrows of moody, grey clouds filled the sky but they weren't nearly as dark as how Dougal felt inside. His oatcake gone, he sat miserably watching groups of settlers lurch round the pitching deck ranting about the conditions aboard the ship. Their mood made him feel worse.

"Ouch!" squealed Janet. Chuckling, she untangled a wisp of her white hair from Wee Mary's tight little fist. "Hey young lady, I need my hair back." The baby giggled and Dougal smiled despite himself. Janet started singing a silly baby song about a mouse. Maggie bopped Dolly about as she joined in.

An extra bagpipe session was what Dougal needed, but as he stood up to go and find Johnny Piper, he felt the first drops of rain. Then the sky opened up.

"Best get yourself below. I'm going to batten down the hatch," said Smiley. "Hold's wet enough without letting more water in. I have to pump it out," he added with a grimace.

"We're staying up here," said Dougal firmly.

Smiley shrugged. "Suit yourself."

Old Hugh lumbered up. "Come on, hen," he said to Janet. "I know it stinks, but we'd best get below. No point getting soaked."

"What about Wee Mary?" fretted Janet. "You know how Morag feels about the children going into that disgusting hold."

"Well, she'll catch her death of cold up here," grumbled Old Hugh.

Dougal took Wee Mary out of Janet's arms and buttoned the baby under his coat. "Don't worry. We'll stay dry under the longboat. Look, the girls are already there. You go, we'll be fine. The wind's strong. We'll sail into better weather soon."

"Well, if you're sure," said Janet reluctantly as Hugh pulled her to her feet. "I really could do with a nap. I hardly slept at all last night with all the groaning and crying going on around us." She followed Hugh down the hatchway.

Dougal handed Wee Mary in to Maggie and was about to crawl under himself when Flora called: "Don't forget to put Mam's cookpot out to catch some water."

"I was going to," snapped Dougal, although he'd totally forgotten. He stood the pot where he thought it would catch the most rain. Smiley was stringing up an old sail to collect the rainwater too.

"Still time to go below," he called.

"We'll be fine out here," said Dougal.

The afternoon was as long and as boring as one of Parson Brown's sermons. The rain got heavier but they were dry enough. Dougal lay on his back watching a spider hurry about on the upside-down bench of the longboat. *He must have come all the way from Scotland*, thought Dougal. *A Scottish spider making the best of things*. The girls played, quarrelled, bickered, and giggled. Dougal ignored them but there was no ignoring Wee Mary once she got hungry.

"Watch your sister," said Dougal. "I'll see if I can find out where Mam's got to." Dougal pulled his coat over his head and made his way to the hatch. It was battened shut, no wonder Mam couldn't come to them. Dougal wasn't able to free the batten with his hands so he gave it a hearty kick.

"Stop that! Young hooligan!" bellowed the Bosun, suddenly appearing with the carpenter by his side.

"My Mam's down there. I've got to tell her the baby needs feeding. Can't you hear her crying?"

"Should have thought of that before. Not opening her up 'til it stops raining. When we close the hatch, it's 'cos it needs to be closed. It stays shut 'til the Captain's say-so," said the Bosun gruffly.

Dougal looked around but he couldn't see the Captain.

"How old's the baby?" asked the carpenter.

Dougal scrunched up his face trying to think. It seemed like they'd been on the ship forever. He could clearly remember the night Wee Mary was born even if he couldn't remember how long ago it was. Her sharp newborn cry had startled him awake in the middle of the night. His Da had stood in the firelight with a bundle of shawls in his big brawny arms.

Dougal had climbed out of his bed and together they'd gone outside to show the new baby her world. It was a clear crisp night and the new moon looked like someone had drawn a smile in the sky. He'd been disappointed at having another sister—how many sisters does a boy need? But he loved Wee Mary to pieces.

"Well?" said the carpenter.

"About four months," calculated Dougal.

"Four months, you say? She's old enough for oatmeal mush then. That's what the wife gives our young'ns."

"Oatmeal mush," repeated Dougal blankly. He returned to the longboat wondering how on earth you made oatmeal mush in the pouring rain.

He picked up his baby sister. "Poor Wee Mary. You're cross 'cos you think we don't understand how hungry you are. Mam can't come 'til the rain stops so we're going to mix some oatcake crumbs with rainwater and you're going to have to make do with that."

Flora and Maggie took turns in crushing and stirring the hard oatcake crumbs. After the longest time the rainwater took on a milky look. Wee Mary spat out the first spoonfuls but in the end her hunger got the better of her and she supped the whole cupful. All the while the rain pounded on the roof and the waves rocked the ship.

The bad weather continued all night and the next day.

"It's never going to stop," whined Flora as the second day drew to a close. Dougal had been thinking the same thing. But a short time later the wind died down and the rain turned to mist.

"There's Mam!" cried Maggie, jigging Dolly up and down.

Mam staggered towards them over the slippery deck. Her clothes and hair stunk of hold-stench but Wee Mary didn't care and almost leapt into her arms.

"How are you feeling?" asked Mam, touching Flora and Maggie's foreheads.

"Bored," said Flora. "There's only us on deck and we've had to stay under the longboat."

"No one ever died of boredom," said Mam, flopping onto the wet deck. Soon Wee Mary was settled and nursing contentedly.

"We've been giving her oatcake mush," said Maggie. "She thinks it's disgusting but she eats it anyway. Dolly thinks it's disgusting too."

"Good," said Mam. "I've hardly any milk now. I'm afraid this will be her last feed from me." She took Flora's hand. "There's something I must tell you and you have to be brave."

Flora became very still.

"Your friends are very sick indeed."

"Are they going to die?"

"We don't know yet." She put her free arm round Flora who buried her face in Mam's chest. Maggie climbed on Mam's knee. "The smallpox is a terrible disease, especially in these conditions and with children so young.

Three more cases showed up yesterday, and two more this morning." Mam's voice cracked and tears dribbled silently down her tired, dirty face. "A little one died of dysentery this afternoon."

Dougal watched Mam and his sisters, and as the terrible things she told them sank in, he wished her arms were long enough to include him in the hug. But he was the man of the family. He had to be strong.

Before Mam could say any more her head drooped onto her chest.

"Let Mam sleep," whispered Dougal. The girls carefully freed themselves from her arms and stood up. Maggie covered her and Wee Mary with a shawl.

"I hope Mam doesn't get sick," said Flora.

CHAPTER 14

ALTHOUGH HE WAS ONLY HALF AWAKE, DOUGAL didn't need to look to know that Mam had gone back to her patients. Maggie whimpered in her sleep, turned over, and was quiet again.

Dougal pulled his jacket tight to keep out the chilly morning air. *It must be August back in Scotland,* he thought, *the hottest time of the year. Wish it was August here.* He was too cold to go back to sleep so he put his hands behind his head and lay thinking about the day ahead.

He'd try and make a fire today, he decided, even if the wood was a bit damp. He'd make Wee Mary some oatmeal and cook up their ration of salt mutton and potatoes. Trouble was, the salty meat made him thirstier than ever and he was only allowed one cup of the murky water a day. It suddenly occurred to him that he hadn't seen Smiley in a couple of days. Later, he'd get the girls to watch Wee Mary and he'd go and find him. Maybe they could fish. A fish dinner was just what his family needed.

Dougal's thoughts were interrupted by a sharp knock on the longboat. He stuck out his head and found the Captain squatting down trying to look under the boat.

"Is that darn Piper under there?" he demanded.

"No, sir. There's just me and my sisters."

The Captain moved his head about, peering into the shadows like he didn't believe him. "Find him and be quick," he said at last. "There's a funeral this morning. We need the pipes. Playing that blessed instrument is the only reason the layabout's on-board. He'd better show himself if he wants to be fed."

The Captain's heavy steps vibrated away.

Leaving his sleeping sisters, Dougal hurried over to Piper Corner. He tried to think how he could get a message to Johnny Piper if he'd gone below.

He needn't have worried. Johnny was there, curled up, facing the side of the ship, clutching his stomach. There was vomit in his hair. He looked and smelled terrible.

"There's been a death. They need you to play for the funeral," said Dougal, gently shaking Johnny's shoulders. "Shall I tell them you're too sick?"

Johnny struggled into a sitting position. "Don't do that. I'll play for a funeral even if I have to be tied to the mast to keep upright."

"I'll fetch some water so you can clean yourself up. You can't play the bagpipes in front of everyone looking like that."

Johnny Piper nodded his head. It seemed like that was all he had the energy for.

In spite of the drizzle the settlers were already gathering on the deck. Some had on their best clothes, but most had struggled up on deck in whatever they were wearing. Dougal skirted round them to the longboat, glad to see that Mam was back.

"Take him these oatcakes," she said, when she heard about Johnny Piper's condition. "He needs food in his belly."

As Dougal hauled up a bucket of seawater, he felt the ship turning sharply. Above him the crew were releasing the sails, letting them flap empty in the wind. This was odd. He lugged the bucket of water and a cloth back to Johnny's nook and took the oatcakes out of his pocket.

Between bites of oatcakes, Johnny stripped to the waist, washed his hands and arms, then dunked his whole head in the bucket of cold seawater. Teeth chattering, but a whole lot cleaner, he dried himself and put his clothes back on. He got to his feet and stood dizzily staring at the sky. "They've stopped the ship," he said. "It's not moving. I'd heard they do that for funerals at sea. Didn't think our Captain would though."

"Do you think you'll be able to play?" asked Dougal.

Johnny Piper straightened his clothes and took the pipes from Dougal. "I'll do the best I can."

Playing as he went, Johnny walked unsteadily over to where the crowd was gathering. A path opened up to allow him through. His melancholy chords seem to understand the settlers' sadness. Fathers hugged mothers, and mothers held their children close. Dougal nodded over to his Mam but stayed near Johnny Piper in case he needed him.

With a face as blank as a mask, the father of the dead child emerged from below deck carrying a small canvas bundle in his arms. The mother came next, weeping like her heart had burst. Janet stepped up to support her. The crowd hushed, the menfolk removed their hats, and

the procession walked slowly round the side of the ship to where the carpenter had balanced a plank between two crates. As the body of the little girl was placed on it, Johnny Piper let the sounds of the pipes fade away.

The Captain took out a weathered prayer book, cleared his throat, and intoned the mournful words of the burial at sea service. Dougal looked across the grey ocean to the grey sky. It was all one big emptiness. He didn't even know which direction Scotland was anymore.

He then glanced over at his Mam, wondering if she was thinking back to Da's funeral. He knew she was. He could hardly bear the sadness of it all, so he scanned the faces for Smiley, but couldn't see him.

"I commit her body to the deep," said the Captain at last. Dougal jerked his attention back to the service. Two sailors lifted the plank to the side of the ship and slowly raised one end. The small white shrouded body gently slipped into the ocean and sank below the waves.

"My baby," wailed the mother. "My poor wee baby." She leaned over the side, arms outstretched, trying to touch the disappearing bag. She would have fallen overboard if her husband hadn't grabbed her round the waist. Maggie trotted to her side and, standing on tiptoes, threw Dolly into the water.

"Why did you do that?" cried Dougal, desperately looking around for something to hook back Maggie's precious rag doll, which was still hovering on the surface.

"I want the baby to have it so she won't be lonely," said Maggie.

The mother broke free of her husband and clasped Maggie to her chest. "You're a wonderful, wonderful, darling wee girl," she said, and clung onto Maggie as tightly as Maggie used to cling onto Dolly. At last Maggie managed to squirm away. The Captain signalled to Johnny Piper to start playing again. But before the first chords had made their way up the pipes, he barked out the orders for the crew to get the *Hector* moving again. Smiley emerged from the hold.

"Where've you been?" asked Dougal.

"Bosun's had me on extra pump duty. Now he needs me up there," he said, tipping his head back to look at the mast. "Sooner be aloft than down in that stink."

Johnny Piper finished a tune, then sank to the ground. "Can't play anymore," he said, panting to get his breath. Mam came over and squatted down beside him. "No fever," she said, feeling his forehead. "But I don't like the sound of your breathing. Probably the dampness. Rest a minute."

Around them the settlers returned to their chores, but the sadness of the day had seeped into every fibre of the ship. Dougal didn't think it would ever go away.

"I feel so bad for the family not having a grave to visit," said Mam. "We can't visit Da but at least we know where he is. The ocean is so cold, so nowhere."

"And there were no flowers," said Maggie.

"I want lots of flowers when I die," said Flora.

"Stop that talk," said Mam sharply. "None of us is going to die for a very long time."

She helped Johnny Piper to his feet and with her arm around him said, "Let's get you back to your corner."

Dougal picked up the bagpipes and was going to follow, but he'd never played the whole instrument before. Here it was all assembled, including the drones, just waiting to be played. He put the bag under his arm and let the three long drone pipes rest across his chest and splay out above his shoulders. They were much heavier than he expected and he had to shuffle his feet to get his balance. He inflated the bag just like he would for a lesson and lowered his elbow to squeeze the air into the pipes. Before his fingers got a chance to play one single note, the drones wheezed an evil scream.

Every eye on deck turned in his direction. The Captain glared and drew his finger across his throat.

Dougal had already stopped blowing and squeezing but it didn't seem to matter. The drones had a will of their own. The excruciating noise continued. Grimacing, folk covered their ears and rushed to the other side of the deck or down the steps into the hold.

"Leave the playing o' the pipes to the piper, laddie," called Old Hugh over the racket.

Johnny Piper hurried back to Dougal, who was holding out the pipes as if they were about to explode. He took them and made the screeches fade away. "Next lesson, I'll show you how the drones work," he said, and started laughing. "You should see your face."

Dougal didn't need to see his face to know it was glowing red from ear to ear. He didn't think it one bit funny, but then he looked at Mam. She was grinning too.

"Oh, Dougal," she said, giving him a hug. "On this day of all days I needed a smile and you gave me one."

"Did you see the Captain's face? It turned bright purple," said Flora, spluttering giggles behind her hands.

"He's not coming over, is he?" said Dougal, pretending to study the mast.

"Too busy," said Johnny Piper.

"Phew! I thought his eyes were going to pop out of his head he was so mad." Dougal forced a laugh, then he said,

"I'm going to light the fire" to change the subject.

Mam didn't stay with them long. She ate some potatoes and broth and had a short nap. As she left to go below, she called out, "And remember—"

"Don't go down into the hold under any circumstance," they chorused. "We know Mam, we know."

CHAPTER 15

"I'M NOT GOING," SHOUTED FLORA. "I'M NOT, I'm not, and you can't make me." Flora squirmed under the upside-down seats to the far corner of the longboat.

"You've got to, they're your friends," said Dougal.

"No they're not, they're dead. How can they be friends if they're dead?" Flora spat out the words and curled herself into a ball.

Even lying out on his stomach with his arms stretched out as far as they would go, Dougal couldn't reach her. The muffled chords of Johnny tuning up his bagpipes slipped in under the longboat and he could see the boots of people gathering for yet another funeral.

"Come out now! I'm meant to be helping Johnny Piper get ready, not crawling around after you."

"Leave her," said Mam.

Dougal startled and knocked his head as he turned in the direction of Mam's voice. She hadn't been above deck for two days. He wriggled out from under the longboat and stood up.

"Poor Flora. It's all too much for her," said Mam, giving him a quick hug. "Seems like there's a funeral every day and this will be the worst one for her."

There had been a lot of funerals and each mournful ritual reminded Dougal of Da's. He only got through them by focusing hard on the bagpipes. If he concentrated on Johnny's fingers and his blowing and squeezing of the bag, the funerals didn't hurt his insides so much.

"The Captain doesn't stop the ship anymore. Have you noticed?" said Dougal.

Mam nodded. "We've got to get to New Scotland as quickly as possible. Twelve bairns have died and there will be more. I know it. The squalor and misery below deck—" she struggled to find the words. "Well, it's worse than anyone could possibly imagine."

Dougal had almost got used to the stench coming up from the hold. Day and night it slipped up through the planking and even the stiff wind that filled the sails couldn't blow it away. Worse still were the cries and screams. The sound of the wind couldn't drown them out either.

"Mam, I want to show you something," said Dougal. He pulled her over to the notches he'd carved on the gunwale, and counted them out loud. "Forty-two," he said. "That means we've been at sea for six whole weeks." Dougal had started scratching circles round groups of seven notches so he could easily count the weeks.

"The voyage is taking much longer than they told us," said Mam. "We'll just have to find our way through each day. When my heart starts sinking, I think of the farm we'll have when we arrive. I imagine fat cows full of milk, and corn growing higher than my head."

"And beans and turnips," said Dougal, remembering last year's garden.

Mam sank down next to Maggie. She took Wee Mary onto her lap, then in a bright voice said, "And how are my girls today?" The baby didn't seem to have the energy to cry much anymore but she managed a tiny smile for Mam.

"I'm your girl too," said Flora, poking her head out.

"Come over here," said Mam.

Flora crawled into Mam's arms and burst into tears.

"Your friends are in heaven, with Da," said Mam.

"But Da doesn't know anything about girls," said Flora, pulling away from her.

Dougal saw Mam's mouth go tight. "He's kind and he knows more than you think."

Dougal didn't like to admit it, but at this moment it wasn't the funerals that were on his mind, it was his growling empty belly and being thirsty all the time. It wasn't like there had been much food back in Scotland, but there was always clean water to drink. The memory of cupping his hands in a fast running stream and drinking gulps of icy cold water whenever he liked made him feel thirstier than ever.

"Do you have this week's rations, Mam?" he asked.

"I do, and it's a lot less than last week. You're going to have to stretch them out. I'm worried about the water. It's going bad. I'm sure that's the cause of much of the sickness."

"We've tried to catch the rain but when it drizzles nothing collects...and last night it poured but the wind knocked over the cookpot and it all got spilled."

"It'll rain again, I guarantee, but for now let's tidy ourselves up and say goodbye to Flora's friends," said Mam.

Mam helped Flora and Maggie wash their faces and smooth out their pinafores. She left as soon as the funeral was over. Dougal handed out the oatcakes, then fed Wee Mary her mush before eating his own. He'd discovered that nibbling it with mouse-sized bites made it last longer, but it didn't really make him feel any fuller. After he'd finished every last crumb he went to pee.

When he came back, the girls were slumped together like shabby rag dolls someone had thrown out. They looked so desperately miserable, especially Flora. She hadn't touched her oatcake. Dougal couldn't believe that he was actually wishing Flora back to her usual brazen self. He tried to think what Da would do. But Flora was right, Da never spent much time with the girls. That was Mam's job. Now there was no Da and no Mam around either. There was just him.

Dougal plodded slowly around the edge of the ship, thinking of things to make Flora smile. She loved having lots of friends to boss about, but the little children were sickly and didn't come on deck to play anymore. Food would make him smile from ear to ear and back again. A huge helping of rabbit stew with lots of potatoes, followed by as many juicy blackberries as he could stuff into his mouth. But there was very little food and none of it was what you'd call good. He was passing his notches for the second time when he got it. Food wasn't Flora's favorite thing, dancing was. Flora was always happiest when she was dancing. They just needed some music, and he knew exactly where to get that.

Dougal ran round to Johnny's corner, losing his balance at the last minute and crashing into the water barrels as the *Hector* lurched over a rogue wave.

Johnny usually slept when he wasn't playing. He said he didn't have any energy to waste. Old Hugh reckoned he was just plain lazy. Sometimes Johnny slept in a long line, sometimes in a C shape, and sometimes scrunched up in a ball. Today he was straight out—a good sign that nothing was hurting.

"Johnny." Dougal gave him a shake. "Johnny, wake up."

"Go away," groaned Johnny, without opening his eyes. "I'm not asleep. How could I be with all the noise you're making?"

"I need some music, right now. Something happy and fast for Flora to dance to. She's desperately sad over losing her friends."

Johnny pulled himself upright. "Are you serious?"

"It's the only thing that will snap her out of her gloom."

Johnny gave him a long hard look. "Everyone's in mourning. It's not like I can play a quiet jig on the pipes."

"Don't remind me," said Dougal, feeling his face heat up. "But she might just fade away, and if she does, Maggie will too."

Johnny looked from Dougal's face to the pipes, snug in their blanket on the deck. "I'll play one song, and I'll leave off the drones so it will be a bit quieter, but I'm warning you this might not go down well."

"We'll risk it," said Dougal, and bounded back to the girls. "We need to clear some space," he said, pushing back a crate and kicking a coil of rope out of the way. Flora and Maggie just sat there. "Sometimes you need to dance and that sometime is now."

Johnny Piper appeared with his bagpipes. "Ta da! Surprise! Johnny Piper's going to play something, just for you." The girls looked blankly at him.

"So you can dance." Dougal bit his lip. They obviously couldn't care less. He was beginning to have serious doubts about his whole plan. If it didn't work he'd be getting Johnny into a heap of trouble, and Mam would give him one of those disappointed looks and ask him how he could be so thoughtless.

He was about to tell Johnny Piper to forget it when the pipes breathed and the music started. It was a tune Dougal hadn't heard before. It was sort of moody but it jiggled too—perfect for dancing. The few settlers up on deck drifted over to listen. Johnny Piper played another tune, faster this time. Feet began tapping. One of the women started stepping a rhythm on the wooden deck.

Dougal watched Flora. She lifted her head and peeked at the tapping boots through her tangle of curls. She couldn't resist. The music started her feet dancing. She twirled, and her hair looked like it wanted to dance right off her head. The tapping boots tapped harder. Flora's feet danced faster, while the crowd whooped and clapped in time to the music. The song ended and Flora collapsed onto the floor in a happy, breathless heap.

Smiley came over. He smelled disgusting and looked like he could fall asleep standing up.

"Where've you been?" asked Dougal.

"In the scuppers working the chain pump! Where else?"

"The ship's leaking badly, isn't it?"

"Seen worse. Don't mind pumping out seawater, it's the stinking muck in the bilge water that gets me! But forget that, I came for some music." He moved into the centre, took a pipe from his pocket, and began to play a tune that got everyone singing.

Johnny Piper played again. Flora didn't stop dancing, even in between the songs when there was no music.
Malcolm and Isobel joined them. Isobel was rubbing
her back. Her baby bump had grown quite big over the
voyage. Old Hugh produced a fiddle. He never did quite
get it in tune but no one cared.

"There's a ceilidh going on up here," yelled one of
the settlers down the hatch. One by one, weary settlers
pulled themselves up the ladder. The strain on their
faces melted away as Johnny Piper played another reel.
Then he started coughing. "I need a break. You play,"
said Johnny, pushing the bagpipes into Dougal's arms.

"Everyone'll jump over the side," said Dougal.
"Remember last time?" The crowd laughed.

"Go on, laddie. Show us what you can do," came a
shout.

Nervously, Dougal placed the bag under his arm.
After running through all the things he had to remember, he played a scale without making a single mistake.
It was a lot easier without the drones. He played the
opening chords of "*Hector*'s Rain Song" and for the first
time, his fingers and mouth and arm seemed to know
exactly what the other was doing. He was having fun
and totally lost count of how many times he repeated
the short riff of chords.

He glanced up to see what the crowd thought of
his playing. The first face he saw was Isobel's. It was
pinched tight, her mouth twisted in a grimace. Dougal's
heart sank. Was his playing that bad? He stopped blowing and let the notes fade away in the middle of the
verse.

"Get your mother," yelled Malcolm, putting his arm
around Isobel.

The crowd shuffled and twittered as Dougal laid the bagpipes down and plodded over to the hatch. He didn't understand. It had sounded pretty good to him. He looked into the dark hole.

"I can't go down there. I'm not allowed below deck."

"Just do it," yelled Malcolm. "Now!"

The twittering and fussing got louder.

"Calm down, everyone, and be about your business," said Janet, waving her hands at the onlookers like they were a swarm of annoying flies. "There's nothing to see here." She put her arm round Isobel's trembling shoulders. "I'll look after Isobel. Malcolm, you go and get Morag. Tell her to bring her bag. Dougal, get the fire going and boil some seawater. If I'm right, the *Hector*'s going to have another passenger very shortly."

CHAPTER 16

B Y THE TIME MAM CAME UP ON DECK, THE
women had shooed away all the menfolk and were
circling Isobel. Balancing herself on the bucking deck
with the wind swirling her skirts, Mam looked around.
"There's no shelter up here, no room to move under the
longboat, and we can't bring a newborn into the world
down in that disease-ridden hold. Where can this baby
be born?"

"Use my corner," said Johnny Piper. "It's not very big
and it's not very warm, but it'll give you some shelter and
privacy."

"I could rig up an old canvas for a roof," added Smiley.

"Do it," said Mam, leading the way with determined
steps.

Dougal lit the fire and eventually the water started
bubbling. Johnny Piper helped him take the steaming
cookpot over to the birthing corner, then they too were
shooed away.

Back at the longboat, Dougal took four small wrinkled potatoes out of their ration supply. "Come on," he said to his sisters. "The fire's hot, we'll bake them in the coals just like we used to do at home."

Johnny Piper sat with Wee Mary in his arms next to Dougal, who poked at the small fire with a stick. They watched the red embers glow and die and glow again while Flora pulled Maggie in skipping circles around them.

An occasional wave splashed up the side to see what was going on, then fell back into the sea. As the *Hector* lumped along, large patches of blue appeared in the sky.

"Choose a cloud," said Flora, squatting by the fireside.

Dougal looked up at the puffy shapes stretching and changing shapes.

"I'm going to choose a bird," piped in Maggie.

"Where's the cloud-bird?" asked Dougal.

"Not a cloud-bird, a real one." She pointed to a gull circling in the distance.

"That's the first bird we've seen since we left Scotland," Dougal exclaimed.

The Captain came by. Johnny Piper and Dougal stood up. "I enjoyed your impromptu concert earlier. What do you people call it?"

"A ceilidh, sir," said Johnny Piper.

"Kay-lee," the Captain repeated. "Well, let's have more of them. Every afternoon, weather permitting. Seems to raise morale to no end." His brows knitted together. "What's going on over there?"

"Isobel McKenzie's having her baby."

"Hmm, I see," said the Captain. He pivoted on his heels and walked briskly off in the direction of his cabin.

Smiley skittered by.

"Has the baby come yet?" asked Flora.

Smiley shook his head. "My Mam was in labour for three days with me. I came out backwards."

"That would account for it," teased Dougal. Smiley punched his arm.

They ate their potatoes under a sky painted in oranges and reds. Dougal could have eaten all four potatoes and still been hungry. He thought by now he'd have got used to the sharp hunger cramps but his body wasn't going to let him forget that it needed more food.

The baby hadn't arrived by the time they went to bed.

Johnny Piper crawled under the longboat with them, and was soon snoring noisily.

"Well, we did what Mam wanted," said Dougal as he changed Wee Mary's napkin and got her comfortable beside him. "We made it through another day, and it turned out to be quite a good one in the end."

~~~

Smiley's loud, exuberant yell woke Wee Mary the next morning. It also woke Dougal. He rolled over, picked up his baby sister, and bounced her on his chest. "I bet the new baby's arrived. Let's go see."

Malcolm was walking the deck, grinning broadly at the blanket-wrapped bundle in his arms. "Here she is," he said, coming over to Dougal. He crouched down and pulled back the blanket. "Isn't she the bonniest baby in the whole wide world?"

Dougal thought the tiny, wrinkled, red face peeking out of the blankets looked a bit like the Bosun on a bad day. But he admired the new baby in the way Mam would have done. From the other side of the ship Smiley let out another loud whoop. "I've got to see what's going on over there," Dougal said, and hurried off.

Smiley and the Bosun were standing side by side in the misty dawn. Every grouchy line on the Bosun's face was turned upwards in an awkward smile as he stared down at Smiley's lead line. The chunk of metal lay on the deck in a puddle of mud and seaweed.

"What's going on Smiley, you fished up some treasure or something?"

"The lead picked up mud from the bottom."

"That all?" said Dougal.

"Means we're in shallower water."

Dougal had no idea why it mattered whether the water was deep or shallow. He actually thought deep preferable—no chance of running aground.

"So?"

"Landlubbers!" With an exasperated huff and a know-it-all eye roll, Smiley said, "Land sits on shelves under the water which means…."

Dougal sucked in his breath. He didn't dare hope for what Smiley was going to say next.

"We're nearing Newfoundland. "

The Captain joined them. "Aye, in a couple of days we'll see her coastline." He looked up at the bulging sails. "If this wind keeps up, maybe less." Relief washed over his face. "This voyage is nearly over. Thank the Lord."

"Amen to that," said Malcolm.

Above the *Hector*, the gulls screeched in welcoming circles. Dougal held his baby sister high above his head. "Did you hear that, Wee Mary? We're nearly there. Only a few more notches and we'll see our new home." The ship lurched and Dougal had to do some quick steps to keep his balance. He pulled Wee Mary back into his arms. "And we'll walk on ground that isn't joggling up and down all the time. Let's go tell your sisters."

"We're nearly there, we're nearly there," sang Flora, dancing off round the deck. Settlers filed up to see the evidence with their own eyes. "Nearly there," they exclaimed to each other. But there had been another death in the night and that meant another funeral.

It turned into a blustery day and the wind blew squalls of rain into the faces of the mourners. It was an adult who'd died this time, but with the news that land was near, the mood wasn't quite as low as it had been at the other funerals. When the service was over everyone wanted to hurry into the dry, but Old Hugh insisted they stay out in the rain while Johnny played a hymn of thanks. For the safe arrival of the new baby and the safe arrival of the *Hector*.

Mam came up on deck for the funeral, then checked on Isobel who was resting in Johnny's corner. "We're calling her Morag after your Mam," said Malcolm, bending down to show Maggie and Flora the tiny baby.

"Our baby sister seems so big now," said Maggie.

"She can nearly sit up all by herself," boasted Flora. "And we're teaching her to dance. We'll teach your baby to dance too."

"She's some growing to do first," laughed Malcolm.

"And we all need to get in out of the rain," said Mam.

"But I like the rain. It's warm and it tastes good too," said Flora, sticking out her tongue.

"No matter, if we get too wet we'll never get dry again. Under the longboat with you now."

Dougal set the cookpot to catch the rain dripping off the sails. Then they huddled with Mam in the dry, chattering about new babies and seagulls and how very soon they'd be in their new home and the awful voyage would be behind them.

CHAPTER 17

"CAN YOU SEE NEWFOUNDLAND YET?" ASKED Dougal, purposely skidding along the slippery deck to where Smiley was staring out over the bow.

"It's only been a day," said Smiley. "If I'd a spyglass or was up top I might see something."

"Why aren't you up there looking out?"

"'Cos I'd get a beating from the Bosun. That's why. Only allowed up top on his whistle. Trust me, you wouldn't want a beating from the Bosun."

Dougal glanced over his shoulder, "No sign of the old buzzard. I'm going up for a look. I was the first one to spot the *Hector*. I'm going to be the first one to spot land."

"Climbin' the mast takes a whole lot of skill. It's not easy, you know."

"Can't be that hard, if you can do it," said Dougal. "My Da used to say I could climb better than a mountain goat."

"Funny, never come across any mountain goats up in the rigging." Smiley snorted with laughter.

Dougal ignored him and looked up at the towering spars. He remembered how back in Loch Broom he knew he could see further if only he could get a little higher. That's when he'd climbed the rocky crag and spotted the *Hector*. It would be the same here. If he could just get a little higher, he was sure he could see land. "Catch me if you can," he yelled and started up the ratline. Smiley scooted over to the other side of the ship and almost ran up the rigging.

Smiley made it look so easy, but it wasn't. Dougal's feet pushed the ladder in while the weight of his body pulled it out. The masts swayed and jerked with every wave so he had to balance as well. It wasn't a bit like climbing the solid granite rocks back home. He climbed up another run trying to ignore the rope burning into his fingers. The ocean was a long way below. He knew he should stop and go back down, but it had been his idea. He couldn't chicken out now.

"One hand for yourself and one for the ship," Smiley shouted across.

Dougal concentrated hard on each body part—hand...hand...foot...other foot...pull up...flatten body...next hand. Dougal's insides prickled with excitement as he started to get the hang of it. Up and up and up he went, thinking about nothing but his hands and feet.

"What kept you?" said Smiley from a small platform above the first cross spar. "Did you stop to milk one of those mountain goats on the way up?"

"Very funny," said Dougal, wedging his body in the ropes. He spread his arms out wide. It felt like he was flying. The wind whistled through the rigging and hushed into the sails, while far below, long rolling waves rocked the *Hector's* stubby hull from side to side. *Johnny Piper'll be throwing up*, he thought.

Smiley started climbing again and Dougal followed. The higher he went the more the mast swayed. He noticed Smiley pausing between each wave, working with the motion instead of fighting it. Dougal tried to do the same.

"Land-ho," screamed Smiley, so loud Dougal startled and nearly lost his footing.

"Where?"

"Over there."

Dougal looked where Smiley was pointing. It was hard to tell cloud from sea, or sky from waves, but as his eyes scanned the ocean he saw the faintest shadow of a line running along the horizon. He hadn't been the first to spot land, but what did it matter? "Newfoundland, here we come!" he cried.

"Land-ho!" hollered Smiley again. He sure could shout. The crew on deck looked up at him—and so did the Captain.

Uh oh! Nobody's meant to know we're up here. We'll be in for it now, thought Dougal. But when he looked down, nobody seemed angry.

"Land to the west," yelled Smiley.

The Captain took out his spyglass and said nothing for a long agonizing minute before he confirmed. "Land in sight."

Cheers erupted from the crew as Smiley slid down the lines. Dougal lowered himself more carefully to the deck. He was sort of disappointed that he hadn't reached the top of the mast and spotted land first, but kind of relieved too. He wasn't as strong as he used to be, and climbing up the rigging would be a whole lot easier if the ship would keep still for a minute.

Dougal peeled himself away from all the excitement to tell Mam, but she'd gone below again. After telling his sisters, he went to find Johnny Piper, who was, as Dougal had expected, vomiting over the side.

"I can't take much more of this," said Johnny Piper, wiping his mouth on his sleeve.

"You won't have to," said Dougal, hopping up and down. "Land is on the horizon. I've seen it with my own eyes. I wish I could go and tell Mam. I know she'll hear, but I want to be the one to tell her."

"I'll tell her," said Old Hugh, who was walking with a spring in his step along the deck with Janet on his arm. "And I'll tell her to pretend I'm you."

"She'll need a mighty big imagination to do that," said Janet, with a chuckle. She let go of Hugh's arm and pulled Dougal aside. Dropping her voice, she said, "Dougal, I don't want to alarm you, but I'm a bit worried about your Mam. She's not well."

Dougal's heart froze. "Has she got the smallpox?"

"Bless yer heart, no," said Janet putting an arm round him. "I didn't mean to scare you, lad. She's not got the pox. It's just she's been working day and night looking after the sick folk down there and she hasn't bothered to look after herself."

"And she's half starved," chipped in Hugh. "Like the rest of us."

"What should I do?" asked Dougal.

"You just go on looking after the family like you've been doing. And I'll do my best to look after your Mam." Janet shook her head. "Though she doesn't listen when I tell her to rest."

"You need to take your own advice, lassie," said Hugh. "You haven't been resting much yourself."

"Stop your fussing, you silly old man," said Janet. "Come, we've a new baby to visit."

Dougal took off his jacket and went about his morning chores with more enthusiasm than usual. He was doing it for Mam. Every time he looked up into the rigging, he relived the excitement of climbing the mast and catching the first glimpse of land.

After their tiny breakfast, Dougal hauled up a bucket of water so they could all have a wash. The air had turned warm and sticky, and washing, even in cold water, felt so good that he stripped Wee Mary off and gave her a soaping and a quick dunk too. She was not impressed but Maggie quickly dressed her back up again and she was soon laughing at her toes.

Flora helped him wash the napkins and string them under the longboat. "They'll dry in no time," said Dougal. "*Ach*, I sound like an old woman!"

Smiley had the fire going in the small brick fireplace and Dougal could smell the salt beef and potatoes cooking. There'd be small portions of weird-tasting, watery stew for dinner but it would be better than oatcakes, which lately had wriggly things in them.

He left Flora and Maggie in charge of the baby and went to find Johnny Piper, hoping to fit in a practice. If it was up to him, he'd play the bagpipes all the way to New Scotland. After all, who knew when he'd get the chance again? But he had his sisters to mind, so a short practice would have to do.

He threaded his way round the settlers straining for their first sight of land. Everyone seemed happy, except the Bosun.

"Don't like it one bit," Dougal overheard him say to the Captain. "Don't like the rollers, don't like the clouds, don't like this heat. We're in the North Atlantic, for cripes sake."

Miserable old buzzard, thought Dougal. *What's not to like about a warm day, especially when the voyage is nearly over.* But when he saw the Captain nodding in agreement, an uneasy twinge sent a shiver up his back.

Curled up in a C with his knees tucked under his chin, Johnny Piper was in no mood to get out the bagpipes.

"Can I borrow the chanter then?" pleaded Dougal. He was desperate to play something. "I'll play somewhere else. I won't disturb you." He took Johnny Piper's groan as a "yes" and brought the pipe back to the longboat. Flora and Maggie skipped off and he played tunes to Wee Mary, who lay on her back, gurgling her own words to the songs.

CHAPTER 18

A S THE AFTERNOON PASSED, DOUGAL FELT THE wind getting stronger. The waves curled with white-caps and splashed up the sides of the old hull. A sudden squall of rain set the folk on deck scurrying in all directions.

Wee Mary began to cry. "Let's go find your sisters," said Dougal, scooping her into his arms and buttoning her under his coat. "Maggie! Flora!"

"We're here," called Maggie, peeking out from beneath a tarp on the far side of the ship. Flora's grinning face appeared beside her.

"I want you two under the longboat."

"It was only a shower and it's fine now," argued Flora. "Don't be so bossy. We might see a rainbow."

"Rainbow? Look at the sky! There's no sun anywhere and it's getting darker by the minute. Get yourselves home, now. There's a storm brewing." It was funny to think of the longboat as home. Dougal held Maggie's hand while Flora dawdled a step behind. Suddenly a wave gushed over the deck in a swirling mass of white foam. Flora slipped and skidded into Maggie who pulled Dougal down with her. Shrieking, they slid across the deck.

Just in time, Dougal managed to stick his feet out and brace himself before crashing into the side of the hull. The wave disappeared through the scuppers and Wee Mary started crying with all her might. Dougal let out a sigh of relief. It was the best sound he'd ever heard. Wee Mary could have been crushed to death—or worse, she could have slipped out of his coat and been washed over the side.

Even though his legs had turned to jelly, he stood up and pulled Maggie and Flora to their feet. "Get to the longboat before the next big wave. Go!" Flora and Maggie scurried ahead, dodging round the last of the settlers filing down the ladder. They crawled into their longboat home and Dougal passed Maggie their crying baby sister.

"Are you mad at me?" asked Flora.

"I'm way more than mad," said Dougal. "How can I keep you safe if you don't mind me? We're in a lot of danger here."

"From now on, we'll to do everything you say, won't we, Maggie?" said Flora.

Maggie nodded her head.

Like that's going to happen, thought Dougal.

"Wee Mary's all wet," said Maggie. Her voice had gone small and trembly.

"We're all wet," said Dougal. "And I don't know how we can get dry."

"I'll change her napkin and give her an oatcake to suck on," said Flora. "Then I'll cuddle her to make her warm."

"I'll help cuddle," said Maggie.

Dougal left them to it and stood up. When he looked over the side, he couldn't believe how strong the wind had grown, and how much the sea had changed in the short time it had taken to collect his sisters. The ocean, now an angry mass of mountains and valleys, tossed the *Hector* around like a toy boat. Waves reared up and smashed over her bows. Dougal spotted Smiley, high in the rigging, struggling to haul in the wild, flapping canvas while the wind did all it could to snatch it away.

He cupped his hands round his mouth. "Be careful up there," he yelled. The masts were swaying wildly, and he was scared that Smiley would plummet to his death any second. Eventually, with the topsails reefed, the rigging crew slid back to the deck. Smiley winked at Dougal, and without missing a beat, got to work pulling down the lower sails. The masts were now completely bare except for one small triangle of sail left at the top. This hadn't happened before in any of the bad weather they'd been through.

Dougal felt the *Hector* slowly turning on an angle with the waves. The ship no longer crashed up and down, but now they were going in the wrong direction. They were heading away from New Scotland!

Dougal crawled under the longboat, and tied Wee Mary to him with Mam's shawl for safety. They all huddled together while the ocean heaved beneath them and the hull groaned in protest at the pounding it was getting. He could feel Maggie and Flora shivering as they clung to him. He was shivering too.

Another rogue wave spread over the deck, sticking its tongue under the longboat.

"I want Mam," whimpered Maggie.

"I'll go find her," said Flora.

"No," said Dougal. "Stay here. What's Mam's rule?"

"Don't go into the hold for any reason at all," chanted Flora and Maggie in squeaky little voices.

"Exactly." But it hadn't been storming like this when Mam had made them make that promise. Dougal thought about Smiley up in the rigging. It must be terrifying up there, but at least Smiley only had himself to look out for. Dougal had three little girls to keep safe. That was way scarier.

Another wave smashed over the deck. They clung on tight to anything they could as it burst under their longboat home, soaking them through before returning to the sea. Dougal looked at the upturned hull. There was no way they could wedge themselves up off the deck. Sitting here, they'd be soaked with every wave. How long would the storm last?

He could see Flora was trying hard not to cry. "The wee mouse ran out of his house," sang Dougal, hoping Janet's mouse song would help. "Come on," he said. "Join in, clap your hands."

"I don't want to sing," sobbed Maggie. "I want my Mam."

And I want Da, thought Dougal, but he tried to keep his feelings of total panic to himself.

"You under there?" A stubbly face with water dripping off appeared under the edge of the longboat. It was the carpenter. "You can't stay out here. There's a hurricane blowin'." He bent his head in and looked around. "Heaven preserve us—you've got little'uns with you."

Dougal blinked back at him. He didn't know what to do—he couldn't stay here and he couldn't go below.

"Next big wave will sweep those young'uns over the

side. You too. Hurry now, pass them out to me and I'll open the hatch for you."

Dougal hesitated. His heart was beating a mile a minute. What should he do?

"Jump to it. There's no time to be hanging about. All the crew's below 'cept me and the Captain."

Dougal made the decision. They'd go into the hold.

"Come on, dearies," said the carpenter, holding out his arms to the girls. Maggie and Flora clung to Dougal tighter than ever.

"Go with the carpenter," said Dougal.

Flora didn't move or lighten her grip one bit. "What about Mam's rule?"

"She'll understand. If we stay here we're all going to drown and...and...Mam will be so sad, she may never ever stop crying. Flora, you're the bravest girl I know. No one is braver than you and if you go, Maggie will go too."

"Really?" asked Flora. "She'll cry for the rest of her life?"

Dougal nodded.

Slowly, Flora released her grip on Dougal's arm. She took the carpenter's hand and wriggled out from under the longboat, pulling Maggie after her.

"There's a girl," said the carpenter. He put Flora under one of his brawny arms and Maggie under the other and carried them to the hatch.

Dougal followed with Wee Mary. "Careful as you..." called the carpenter. "It's like...wal...ice." The howling wind snatched away his warnings. Dougal didn't need them. He had no idea how a little ship could survive in such a terrible sea. He waited until the next wave left the deck, then, leaning into the wind, he struggled towards the hatch.

The carpenter put Flora and Maggie on top of the ladder, then helped Dougal take the last few steps across to the hatchway. As soon as they were all down in the hold, he slid home the hatch cover. It was complete and utter blackness. For a moment, the sound of the latches clicking into place drowned out the sounds of the storm and the wails of the settlers.

CHAPTER 19

DOUGAL COULDN'T BREATHE IN THE SUFFO-cating blackness. *It must be like this in Da's coffin*, he thought, and a chill slithered down his back. Quickly, he turned his attention to Flora and Maggie who were clinging to his legs like barnacles on an old wharf.

The *Hector* pitched upwards, sending a wave of foul smelling slime sloshing around their knees. Then she slammed down and the gruesome muck raced away only to return with every shake and shudder of the hull. Something flew across the passageway and splashed into the bilge water. The screams and shrieks from the settlers swelled, then faded as the *Hector* stabilized. They increased with renewed terror as she rocked on her side and rose up again.

Dougal grabbed tight to a post. He heard Maggie retching, then Flora throw up. Hard as he tried, he couldn't take the stench and spiralling motion either. He bent over and threw up too.

It was so dark that even when Dougal's eyes adjusted he could still only make out shadowy patches in the filthy blackness. *Everyone on the ship's down here,* he thought. *Old Hugh and Janet, Malcolm and Isobel with their new baby, the stone-throwing boys, Flora's friends, Johnny Piper, sick settlers, well settlers, the Bosun, Smiley and the rest of the crew, my sisters, and our Mam. But it feels like there's just me.*

"Mam," called Maggie. "Where are you?"

"MAM," yelled Flora, "WHERE…ARE…YOU?"

"Stop!" said Dougal. "She can't hear you above all this noise, so there's no point wasting your energy. Mam'll be in our bunk at the other end of ship. We'll go to her but I can't move with you both clinging to my legs." He remembered Smiley's instruction from when they were climbing the rig. "I'm going to need one hand for the ship, or we'll all fall over. Maggie, you hold my hand, and Flora, hold onto my coat, really tight. And whatever you do don't let go. Understand?"

"Yes," said Flora.

"I can't see you, so I need to hear you," said Dougal.

"Yes," shouted Flora and Maggie.

"Good."

Every slam and crash of waves against the old hull sent belongings flying and settlers screaming. The terror in their wails sounded more like the death throes of a wounded beast than the cries of individual people. Someone started to sing a hymn. Others joined in.

Dougal began to notice a rhythm in the movement of the ship. He got a sense of when he'd be able to move forward and when he should stop and hang on for dear life.

His breath was coming in quick gasps. "Da, please help me keep them safe. Please don't let them fall, 'cos I won't be able to see to find them," he said. "Oh, and don't let anything hit us as we walk along. Let's go girls."

One slow, nerve-racking step at a time he felt the way forward, stopping and grabbing on to whatever he could when the movement was most violent, moving on when the *Hector* tipped in the right direction. A sudden lurch slammed him against a bunk frame. He tightened his grip round Maggie's hand and made sure he could still feel Flora's tug on his jacket. Stumbling over debris in the bilge water, he moved forward again. A box flew past his ear. This dark journey down the length of the ship was the longest he'd ever taken in his life.

He stopped. They couldn't go any further. They'd arrived at the end curtain. The one Dougal had peeked round when he'd first seen the leaking hull. Someone was there cranking the chain pump but he couldn't see who.

"This is our bunk," said Dougal. He felt for the ladder and boosted Flora up.

"Mam's not here," she shouted.

Oh no, thought Dougal. *Did we come along the wrong gangway?* "Is anyone up there?" he called out to Flora.

"No, but Mam's shawl is here. I know it's hers, it still smells of lavender."

"It must be our bunk then," said Dougal.

"I want to smell Mam's shawl," said Maggie.

"Hang on," said Dougal. The ship lurched and he gripped Maggie's wrist tightly until the floor levelled. He was about to boost her up when he said, "Wait! Flora, see if there's a rag to wipe our legs. We need to keep our bunk as clean as we can. That's what Mam would do."

"It does smell of lavender," said Maggie, when, with feet wiped, she'd scrambled into the bunk. It was awkward moving with Wee Mary, but somehow Dougal got himself up into the bunk too.

Every wave buffeted them against each other but at least they were out of the storm, and out of the muck. Dougal also hoped that in their bunk behind the curtain they'd be safe from the poxes and germs. He kept Wee Mary tied to him even though she was complaining loudly. It was hard to move even a little but he couldn't risk her being jolted out.

"I don't like the dark," whimpered Maggie. "It feels like I'll never ever see again."

"You'd like it if you were a mole," said Flora.

"I'm not a mole."

"You could pretend to be a mole."

They burrowed under Mam's shawl and soon the wriggling stopped and they fell asleep. Dougal didn't dare let himself go to sleep, he needed to keep watch. As he lay listening to the raging fury of the storm, he wondered what it was like up on deck and if he'd be more scared if he could see the *Hector* battling the ocean. He was exhausted but daren't let his eyes close. It was too dangerous and he needed to be awake for his sisters. But he did fall asleep. He couldn't help it.

Some time later, Dougal was awakened by Wee Mary. He then dozed off again and woke again. It was so hard to keep track of time in the darkness. After a while he had no idea if a night had gone by or a whole other day.

"When's it going to end?" sobbed Maggie. "I miss Dolly. She's never afraid."

"Hug Mam's shawl," said Dougal. "It's full of warm happy thoughts."

"I'm really thirsty," said Flora.

Dougal felt the same way.

Slowly, he realized the ship wasn't bucking so much. Maybe the storm was over.

"Rations!" a familiar voice called out in the dark. "Get your cups ready!"

Dougal pulled back the curtain. "Smiley! Am I pleased to see you!"

"Hey mountain goat friend. Here, take these." He passed in some oatcakes. "Make them last. I don't know when I'll be round again. Hold out your cups. I've got rainwater."

"Oh no! We left them on deck," said Dougal.

"Cup your hands and I'll give you each a splash and see if I can get back to you later." He tried to give Wee Mary some but much of it spilt out of her mouth.

"Looks like the storm's nearly over," said Dougal, after he'd gulped down his handful of water.

"Dream on," said Smiley. "We're bang smack in the middle. Us sailors call it the eye of the storm. There's a whole lot more to come. Hold out your hands, I'll give you each another splash."

"Have you seen our Mam?" asked Dougal.

"Expect she's helping some poor soul weather the storm. Don't know what sick folk'd do without her."

"If you see her, tell her we're all safe," said Dougal.

"Will do," said Smiley, and went about his rounds.

By the time they'd eaten their oatcakes the storm had returned. It was like somebody had opened a door and let all the wild weather back. The shrieking and screaming resumed. Maggie and Flora were doing their share. Nothing Dougal said made any difference.

As he tried to get more comfortable, something jabbed Dougal in the ribs. It was the chanter, still in his pocket. He pulled it out and, lying on his back, started to play. Just a few notes, not even a tune, but the notes seem to make up their own music. Soon Wee Mary stopped crying, then Flora and Maggie slowly quieted too. Dougal kept playing, letting the simple melody push away the bad sounds outside their bunk.

CHAPTER 20

"DOUGAL, WAKE UP! IT'S MORNING!" MAGGIE was pounding on his chest.

Dougal opened his eyes. The blackness had turned to greyness. He pulled aside the curtain and saw light streaming through the open hatch cover at the other end of the ship. Maggie was right, it must be morning or afternoon. "The storm's over," he said. "We made it through."

Flora and Maggie began bouncing up and down. Wee Mary started crying.

"Stay still you two. You'll wreck the bunk and you're scaring Wee Mary. I want to see what's going on."

There was a buzz of cussing and praying as, one by one, the settlers realized the nightmare was over. Some headed for the ladder. Others re-lit the oil lamps and bumbled about searching for possessions thrown around by the storm.

"Let's get out of here," said Dougal.

"I want my Mam," wailed Maggie, for the millionth time.

"She'll be looking for us under the longboat, right this minute. Come on. Let's get back on deck and find her." They climbed down from the bunk and Dougal led the way through the filthy, stinking bilge water.

"It's disgusting," said Flora.

"Don't look down," said Dougal.

"I feel sick," said Maggie.

"Mam'll be really mad you brought us down here in all this muck," said Flora. "We're going to get sick. I'm going to tell her it's all your fault, Dougal. You made us break her rule."

"We're going up now, aren't we?" snapped Dougal.

Bumping round bits of debris and other settlers blocking the passageway, they eventually made it up the ladder.

"Woah!" cried Dougal, as his head poked through the hatch. "Will you look at all that mess?"

"Move along," said a settler. "There's more of us behind wants to get on deck."

"Sorry," said Dougal. He quickly pulled Flora and Maggie up. With gaping mouths, they looked around. Splintered boxes, tangled ropes, and bits of seaweed were strewn everywhere.

"That was one heck of a storm," he heard someone say.

"Didn't think this old tub could take such a beating, and that's the truth," said another voice. "She's still got her masts too."

Dougal looked up to check. Yes, they were still there, and against the brilliant blue sky he could see Smiley hanging over the yardarm, letting down the sails.

"There's the quilt Mam made me," said Maggie. She ran over and started tugging the saturated piece of bedding back to the longboat, which had swung sideways and was pointing into the centre of the ship.

"Mam's not here," said Flora, accusingly. "You said Mam would be here."

Dougal didn't know how to answer her. He had absolutely no idea where Mam was. He untied Wee Mary from his chest and handed her to Maggie. Then he stretched his back which was aching from having had the baby tied to him for so long. He took the remainder of the oatcakes that Smiley had given them from his pocket and handed them around.

"But where's Mam?" asked Maggie again.

"I don't know," said Dougal, louder than he intended. Maggie burst into tears. Flora threw her arms round her.

"We don't like you, Dougal Cameron, and we're not going to talk to you anymore."

"Fine by me," said Dougal. "I've had enough of you two." He stormed off. He was fed up with being a Mammy to the girls. Da never had to look after them night and day, that was Mam's job. But where was Mam? They hadn't passed her on their way to the ladder and there was no sign of her up on deck.

She's here somewhere and I'm going to find her, he decided, and climbed down the ladder into the hold.

He started at the very back, a section they wouldn't have passed when they came up on deck. "Mam," he called out as he walked along, knocking at the frames of every curtained bunk. "Mam, are you in there?"

"Your Mam's in this one," said Janet suddenly appearing out of nowhere. She pulled aside the curtain.

Dougal gasped.

Stringy hair tangled about the thin white face of the woman lying on the bunk. Dried spit crusted around her mouth. Was this really Mam? She didn't look like Mam at all. When did she get so sick? The days had all mushed into each other so he couldn't even remember if the last time he saw her was the day before the storm or the day before that.

"Hello, Mam," he whispered, bending over the bed. Mam's breath smelled foul. There was no reaction and he wasn't sure if she'd recognized him. "Mam! It's me, Dougal. We're all safe, even Wee Mary." At Wee Mary's name, Mam's eyes glared out of their dark hollows.

"Get away from me. You know the rule," she said, in a hoarse, angry whisper.

"But Mam…the storm…."

Janet put her hand on his shoulder. "It's the fever talking. She just wants you to be safe."

"She'll get better?" asked Dougal. "She'll be our Mam again?"

Janet hesitated. "If the fever breaks soon," was all she would say.

Dougal turned to his Mam. "Come up top. We'll look after you. Fresh air and a hug from Wee Mary will make you better in no time."

"In a little while," said Mam. Her eyes drooped closed. "I need to rest."

"No! Don't close your eyes. Stay awake," pleaded Dougal.

Janet let the curtain fall. "Go to your sisters. Your Mam's right, you'll catch something if you stay down here. Your sisters need you healthy. Right now you're all they've got."

But Dougal didn't want to go back to his sisters. He was still mad at them. He wanted Mam to look after them. He also wanted Mam to look after him.

Clambering over the debris on deck, he went to his line of notches. Before carving the new notches he counted the ones that were already there. Fifty-six! *That can't be right.* He counted again and got the same number. Had they really been at sea for eight weeks?

While he was counting, the Captain came on deck with his sextant. *Must be noon*, thought Dougal. He didn't know how the shiny brass instrument worked. Smiley couldn't explain it either, he just knew that if the Captain took readings at mid-day he could tell where the ship was. At night he used the stars. Dougal thought that was really clever 'cos with no hills or lakes, how could you possibly know where you were? He wondered if Da knew about sextants. He probably knew a lot about stars by now.

With a frown, the Captain returned to his cabin. Curious, Dougal snuck up and looked in the window. After poring over his charts, the Captain folded them up and sat with his head on his hands. When he stood up, his frown was so deep his eyebrows joined together. Dougal ducked down as the Captain came out of his cabin. Hollered orders were passed along the ship. The crew immediately stopped cleaning up and hauled on ropes to reset the sails. Dougal felt the *Hector* change direction.

Folks gathered on the deck, crowding the Captain with their questions. He held up his hands for quiet. The crowd hushed.

"Fellow travellers, we must give thanks that we have survived as ferocious a storm as I have ever encountered in all my years at sea."

A faint cheer rose from the crowd.

"As you see, the masts are intact and the *Hector* sustained no serious damage," continued the Captain. "The carpenter is already at work making any needed repairs to the hull. I have given orders for the chain pump to be in operation round the clock."

That's not right, thought Dougal. The Bosun had started the pump going as soon as he'd discovered the leak at the very beginning of the voyage.

There was an uneasy shuffling. Everyone seemed to sense that whatever the Captain had to say next would not be good.

"Unfortunately…" *Here it comes*, thought Dougal. The Captain cleared his throat. "The storm has blown us a considerable way off course."

"How far off course?" called Old Hugh.

"By my calculations, it will take us two weeks to regain our position."

"Two whole weeks! You can't be serious," yelled a voice, breaking the heavy gulp of silence that had followed the Captain's statement.

"I insist you turn this ship around immediately and take us back to Scotland," shouted a man, punching the air with his fist. Soon the rest of the settlers were chiming in as well.

"Aye, take us back to Scotland! We want to go home!" "Hear! Hear!" "This voyage has been a disaster!" "We can't go on like this." "How many more of our children will die?" "We have to go back." "This voyage is doomed!" "Take us home." "My wife's at death's door."

Death had a door! Dougal hadn't known this.

The clamouring got louder. Seemed everyone wanted to go back to Scotland. Dougal didn't know if he wanted to go back or forward. Scotland was home and familiar, but they had nothing there anymore. Everything had been sold. In Nova Scotia there'd be a farm to work, but without Mam there'd be no farm. Janet's words came back to him. "You're all they've got." And he realized his sisters were all he had, too.

The Captain was speaking again. "I have been commissioned to take you to New Scotland and that is what I intend to do. Good day to you all." With a face like thunder, he marched back into his cabin.

Dougal raced back to the girls. Suddenly he didn't want them out of his sight. He picked up Wee Mary and hugged her close even though she was kicking and not wanting to be held at all.

"We're still not talking to you," said Flora, turning her back on him.

"I've found Mam," said Dougal.

Flora whipped round.

"She's sick."

"You mean dying sick?" said Flora, tears threatening to race down her cheeks.

"No," said Dougal, quickly. "She'll come up on deck when she feels better. She said she loves you and you have to be good and do everything I tell you without whining and whingeing."

"No she didn't," said Flora, laughing and crying at the same time.

"Come here," said Dougal. He opened his arms and hugged his grimy, annoying sisters. "Right now we've only got each other, so we have to look after each other. Agreed?"

The girls nodded.

"I didn't think you were going to come back," sobbed Maggie and hugged Dougal even tighter.

"I won't ever leave you. I promise," said Dougal. "And I'll try not to be so bossy."

The hugging continued. "But you can let go of me now. First, we've got to get our boat home back in place," said Dougal. He went over to the longboat and pushed against one end with all his might.

"You need help," said Flora. "Come on, Maggie."

"Heave away ho!" chanted Flora, just like the crew did when they were all pulling together.

"I think she's starting to move," said Dougal, as the heavy longboat slowly nudged back to where it was supposed to be.

"There, we've got our home again," said Dougal. "Maggie, can you see to Wee Mary? How you're going to get her dry I don't know. Flora, you go round and collect up our belongings. They're scattered everywhere."

Surprisingly, the girls did as they were told. Flora tugged back the quilt and Dougal squeezed it out. He caught the water in Mam's big cookpot. It looked a bit murky but no worse than the water Smiley handed out. He took a mouthful then sprayed it out. "Blahhh! It's salty. I thought it'd be rainwater and we could drink it. Still, at least we can wash Wee Mary in it," he said.

As they draped their wet stuff over the top of longboat to dry in the sun, bagpipe chords floated over the deck. Dougal expected Johnny Piper to appear but the music stayed distant.

"Back in a minute," said Dougal. He hurried over to what was left of Piper Corner. The water barrels were on their sides. One had split right open, another had rolled away. Johnny Piper was sitting on the ground examining his pipes.

"Did you stay here during the storm?" asked Dougal.

"'Course not," said Johnny Piper. "I went below with the crew. But the pipes got soaked even in the hold. I was checking them out. They seem all right. It's not like it doesn't rain in Scotland." He stroked the hide bag. "These old pipes have seen a lot of hardship. No doubt they'll see a lot more before they're done."

"Keep playing," said Dougal.

CHAPTER 21

DOUGAL WAS HUNGRY. SO HUNGRY HE COULD have eaten a whole whale and still had room for some rabbit stew. He shuffled his feet along the deck, adding dumplings and all sorts of other foods to his imaginary meal. Just walking the deck took a lot of energy, but he had to carve his morning notches. They made him feel like they were getting somewhere. Without them the days would join together and it would be like they were just bobbing up and down. Perhaps that's all they were doing.

Smiley was sitting by the gunwale a few feet away. The frayed old lead line hung loosely over the side of the ship and drooped across his knees.

Dougal licked his cracked lips before calling out: "That's…" his voice didn't come out at first. He tried again: "That's two weeks of notches since the storm. We must be getting close to New Scotland by now. Any more seaweed?"

"Dunno." Smiley sniffed and wiped his nose on the back of his hand. "I can't get the lead up onboard. I've tried and tried. My arms haven't got any pull left in them."

"Seems like you need the help of a mountain goat," said Dougal, although he wasn't sure he had enough strength to be of any use. He took hold of the rope anyway. "Okay. Together, ready?"

Smiley sniffed again. "Ready."

"Heave away ho! And again, heave away! She's coming up, I can feel her moving! Start counting the knots, Smiley." The rope inched aboard then the lead cylinder suddenly broke the surface, becoming heavier as it hovered above the water. Dougal quickly stepped on the rope to stop the cylinder falling back into the ocean. "One more pull."

The lead cylinder bumped over the gunwale and thunked onto the deck. Dougal fell back and lay there panting to get his breath. He looked over at Smiley, expecting him to be laughing his head off, but Smiley wasn't smiling. Dougal had never seen him look so down.

"Well?" said Dougal.

"Less knots than yesterday," said Smiley.

"That's good isn't it? Means we're nearly there."

"About two more days to go," said Smiley.

Dougal had seen a thin purple shadow of land the day before, and it was definitely bigger this morning. He could even see its shape. "Don't tell me there's another storm coming?"

Smiley shook his head. "Worse."

"Can't think of anything worse than the storm we went through."

"No food or water. That's worse than any storm."

Dougal's eyes narrowed. "What are you saying?"

"Food's all gone, every bit of it. The voyage has taken too long, there's nothing left—not a single mouthful of anything.

"No water either?" asked Dougal.

"Seawater got into the last of the water barrels. They got cracked in the storm."

Dougal's belly growled loudly and painfully like it understood every word Smiley had said. "Nothing left at all?"

"Not a crumb. Bosun's telling the folks below now."

Dougal stared out over the never-ending ocean. It was a sparkly blue-green today. How could it look so beautiful when things were so bad? He was desperately hungry and the thought of no food for two more days was unbearable. "I have to get back to the girls. You know what Wee Mary's like if she doesn't get…." He gasped. "What am I going to give Wee Mary? She can't survive on nothing for two days!"

"Don't suppose there are any crumbs on the blanket?" asked Dougal when he crawled under the longboat to join his sisters. Wee Mary was whimpering, her feet and arms pumping the air as Maggie battled to change her napkin.

"Crumbs!" exclaimed Flora. "We never leave crumbs anymore."

"I know. But…" Dougal took a deep breath. "Smiley just told me there's no more food on-board."

"We'll starve to death," said Flora in a high-pitched squeal. "I'm starving now."

"I'm starving too," said Maggie. "And Wee Mary will starve to death. I don't want Wee Mary to die."

"Stop!" said Dougal. "No one's going to die!" Maggie's bottom lip started to wobble. "I'm sorry, I didn't mean to shout. Look at me. We're nearly there. We can hang on just a little longer. We survived the hurricane didn't we?"

The girls nodded solemnly.

"We can survive this. We'll think of something."

They sat side by side against the longboat. Dougal took Wee Mary onto his lap. Soon, she was asleep. It seemed she was asleep more than awake these days. This worried Dougal. He watched the settlers drifting by. The sun was shining and the wind ruffled his hair. It was a morning very like the first one of the voyage, except the folk walking about moved in slow motion and there were no games, no chasing around, no laughter. Even the muttering was hushed, as if talking out loud used up too much energy. He looked at the sky, hoping for a rain cloud to bring a mouthful of watery relief.

"Old Hugh will be up soon to tell us how Mam's doing," said Dougal, turning his attention back to his sisters. "Remember how much better he said she was yesterday?"

Maggie started pulling excitedly on Dougal's coat. "Old Hugh has food. Don't you remember how we used to laugh because he was always collecting up scraps of old oatcakes?"

"They were disgusting then, they'll be inedible now," said Flora.

"Still food," said Dougal. "But this voyage has gone on so long, I'm sure he'll have tossed them overboard by now."

It seemed ages before Old Hugh's bald head emerged from the hatch.

They raced over, then stopped in their tracks. "Mam!" shrieked Maggie and Flora, jumping up and down. Mam, assisted by Janet, was coming up the ladder behind Old

Hugh. Dougal leaned over and grabbed hold of her arm to help her up the last steps. As she stepped on deck, the girls ran to her and they all hugged and hugged. Dougal worried they'd break every bone in Mam's terribly thin body. He kept hugging anyway.

"Enough!" bellowed Old Hugh. "Give the poor woman some space. She needs to sit down."

"Your lovely faces," said Mam, over and over. Tears dripped down her cheeks as she let herself be pulled along. "And the blue sky. I didn't think I'd ever see any of this again." Once she was comfortably seated, she took Wee Mary into her arms. "You poor, skinny darling."

"There's no more food," said Flora. "Unless…" she turned to Old Hugh. "Do you still have the oatcake scraps you collected?"

"Aye, I do, lassie. I knew there'd come a time. Didn't I always say about not wasting food, Janet?"

"You did, and you were right," his wife answered, indulgently. "Except there's over a hundred and fifty souls on-board and I don't see how we can feed that many mouths with one sack of mouldy oatcakes. There's not even enough to feed all the children."

"Oatmeal mush," said Maggie.

"You're brilliant, Maggie!" cried Flora.

Janet looked puzzled. Flora explained. "We crush oatcakes up in water to make a mush for Wee Mary. A pot of mush will feed more people than little pieces of oatcakes."

"Porridge," said Old Hugh, in a loud triumphant voice. "That's exactly what us Scots need." He turned to Smiley. "Get the fire going, laddie, and boil whatever water you've got. Even if it's briny, it won't be as salty as the ocean. I'll get the oatcakes."

They all moved across to the fireplace and Smiley, using debris from the storm, soon had a fire crackling. More settlers gathered round when they heard what was happening. Three big cookpots were set to boil. Old Hugh brought up the oatcake scraps and set Dougal and Flora to bashing the sack with a chunk of wood to break up the bigger pieces.

"Enough already," he called, and divided the contents of the sack into the bubbling pots of water.

"Smells like the hold," said Dougal, giving the lumpy green mixture some brisk stirs with his sack-bashing spar.

"Something's wriggling on the top," said Smiley.

"Put a handful of grubs in for protein," Old Hugh whispered, tapping the side of his nose. "Best not tell the womenfolk."

Dougal grimaced, but his belly told him it'd be happy for anything he'd like to throw its way, and that included bugs.

"Probably tastes worse than it smells but it's better than starving," said Old Hugh with a smug chuckle.

"Make sure you boil it well," Mam called over. "Boil off those germs. That's important."

"Stop fussing, Mam," said Flora. "You're meant to be sitting still, getting better."

"Yes," said Maggie, repositioning the shawls round Mam's shoulders.

"My, you're a bossy pair. Wait a minute, I do believe there are still some herbs left in our sea chest. They'll add a bit of flavour. I'll go and get them."

"Oh no you won't," said Old Hugh. "You stay where you are. I'll send the lad for them."

Dougal soon returned with the herbs and stirred them into the mix. Then a settler produced a small wrinkled potato that she'd found in her bunk. A few other people searched around the corners of their bunks and came up with other long forgotten dried up old vegetables. They were cut up small and put in the cookpots.

"Is it porridge or soup?" asked Maggie.

"It's porridge-soup," said Flora. "Porroup."

The sun was high in the sky. *It must be noon*, thought Dougal, as the Captain came out of his cabin and took his sextant measurements.

"Get your mugs, the porridge is ready," shouted Old Hugh. "Make a line, children and crew first. If the crew gets too weak to sail the ship, we're all doomed."

The Captain came over and watched Janet dole out the porroup. "I think there's enough for a full ladle for everyone on-board. Have you your cup, sir?" she asked.

"Thank you ma'am," said the Captain. "Much obliged for your efforts." He took a sip of the steaming liquid. "This has to be the most disgusting thing I have ever tasted in my whole life," he said with a smile, "but it will see us through. Folks, can I have your attention? By my latest calculations, we'll be in New Scotland some-time tomorrow."

A cheer went up and smiles appeared on the weary, grey faces. "We need some music," someone called out. "Where's that Johnny Piper fellow?"

"Never around when we need him."

"Well, we'll surely need him tomorrow," said Old Hugh. "He'll be piping us off the ship and onto Nova Scotian soil."

"We must all put on our best shawls and bonnets," chattered the women.

"And our plaids," added another settler.

Where was Johnny Piper?

CHAPTER 22

DOUGAL WAS ALMOST TOO EXCITED TO GO TO bed that night. He stayed looking over the bows until it got dark. The purple shadow was now very much land. It was green and brown and grey. The sky was clear, the wind was good, and they were getting closer to it every minute. Dougal couldn't wait to step ashore.

"I didn't know there were that many trees in the whole world," exclaimed Flora the next morning. "And I didn't know trees could grow that big. They're as tall as mountains and as wide as our croft." She was standing on her tiptoes next to Dougal, watching the land get nearer and nearer. As the *Hector* lumped towards the mouth of a sheltered harbour, Dougal shifted Wee Mary onto his other hip, took out his flint stone, and carved the very last notch of the voyage.

"Number seventy-seven. We've been at sea for eleven whole weeks!"

"I can't remember not being at sea," said Flora, scrunching up her face to think. "I can't even remember what our old home looked like."

"But you do remember Da," said Dougal.

"'Course."

Dougal didn't think she sounded very sure, so he changed the subject. "Well, we're here now. Look, Wee Mary. There's Nova Scotia."

"Nova Scotia!" Flora tasted the word. "I like the sound of that name."

They weren't alone. Everyone was up on deck, craning their necks to get a view of something other than sea. Little children were hoisted onto shoulders while the bigger kids climbed on whatever they could. No one wanted to miss this first sighting of their new homeland.

"Where are the fields? That's what I want to know," grunted Old Hugh. "All I can see are these hulking great trees. Cannae grow crops and graze cows in a dang forest."

"Must be inland a bit," said Janet, bending and stretching to see if she could view any farmland through the tree trunks.

"Doesn't smell right to me," Old Hugh grumbled. Behind him, Dougal could hear other men rumbling their own complaints. But at this moment he couldn't care less about farms or forests. He just wanted to walk on dry land and get some food in his belly. Seeing as the Bosun wasn't around, he decided to climb the ratlines for a better look at his new homeland. But before he got a chance to pass Wee Mary to Flora, he heard Maggie calling.

"Dougal, come quick. Mam needs you."

Dougal got back to the longboat as fast as he could and saw immediately why Mam wanted him.

"The longboat's to be turned over and turned over now," thundered the Bosun. "So get yourselves out the way. Wouldn't have let you sleep under there in the first place if it'd been up to me."

"At least give us some time to get our things together," said Mam. "The *Hector* hasn't even dropped anchor yet."

"Now!" said the Bosun. "My men've got a ton of things to do and the longboat's in the way."

"Very well." Mam's face reddened. "Impossible man," she hissed under her breath.

Dougal helped her stand up. "Mam, take it easy or you'll get sick again. Sit over here with Wee Mary and we'll bring everything over. We can do it fast, can't we girls?"

Flora and Maggie dove under the longboat and threw out the clothes, shawls, and blankets. Dougal ran and dumped them in a heap where Mam was sitting and returned for another armful.

"Don't forget my cookpot," called Mam, "and maybe Smiley could get our sea chest up from the hold."

"I think he's a bit busy at the moment," laughed Dougal, pointing skywards to where Smiley was furling the topsails.

"There's so much to do," fussed Mam. "Apart from getting packed up, we need to tidy ourselves. I think seagulls have made nests in the girls' hair." Flora and Maggie collapsed in a fit of excited giggles. "Oh, and Dougal, the Captain has charged us with getting Johnny Piper ready. He wants him cleaned up so he can pipe us onto land. If Johnny Piper's to be at the front, he's got to look his best."

"I'll find him, Mam, but take it easy, you're still sick. We can manage, you know."

Mam smiled. "You really are becoming the man of the family."

Dougal was smiling too as he bumped his way through the bustling clusters of settlers. Everyone was packing up and getting in the way of the crew, to the Bosun's extreme annoyance. But even the Bosun's fiercest scowls and curses couldn't spoil the mood or keep the older kids from climbing the rigging.

Dougal's smile vanished when he reached Johnny Piper. Johnny was slumped over, with his head on his knees. His precious bagpipes lay in a knotted muddle at his feet. "What's the matter?" said Dougal, shaking the piper's shoulder gently.

Johnny Piper sat up, then, gasping for air between each word, said, "Don't...worry about...me...look after...my bag...pipes...." He clutched his chest and coughed and coughed.

"Stay still. I'll sort them out."

The piper leaned back against a pile of crates and closed his eyes. Every breath was a painful wheeze. Dougal carefully set about the mess of strings and pipes, laying each part straight as soon as he'd untangled it. "We've arrived, Johnny, and everybody's getting ready to leave the *Hector*. We're all going to wear our best clothes and you'll be playing the bagpipes as we step onto Nova Scotia soil for the first time. Won't it be grand?"

Johnny Piper's face looked even more miserable than before. "If...I...c...can't breathe...I can't...blow."

Dougal had already realized this. "I'll take you to Mam. She's not well herself, but I'm sure she'll be able to do something. Here, stand up. Lean on me."

"Bring my pipes."

As they made the slow trip across the deck, Dougal noticed all the sails were down. Then just as they reached Mam, the command to "drop anchor," rang out. Smiley brushed by. "We're getting up stuff from the hold next. I'll bring your sea chest over," he called without stopping.

"Sit down here, Johnny," said Mam, patting the deck beside her. Dougal could tell by the look on her face that this was serious. "Did Dougal tell you about our grand arrival?" she asked while her fingers examined Johnny Piper's head and neck. She put her ear against his chest. "Deep breath, please."

"Aye, he did," said Johnny Piper.

Mam finished her examination. Dougal could see she looked worried.

After another bout of coughing subsided, Johnny Piper turned to Dougal. You...must be...the piper."

"Me?" Dougal gulped. "But the bagpipes still squawk in all the wrong places when I play, and I haven't practiced since before the storm and that was two weeks ago."

"It's you or nobody," said Mam. "Johnny can't possibly play in his condition. Folk will be sorely disappointed if there are no bagpipes, on this day of all days. The bagpipes are a symbol of...how can I put it? Freedom and how we want to live."

"Hey, mountain goat, here's your sea chest," Smiley puffed up and dropped the end of the wooden box he'd been dragging with a bang on the deck.

"Thanks, Smiley," said Mam. "For bringing up the sea chest and for everything you've done for us on this horrific voyage."

"My pleasure." He was about to run off when Mam called him back. "Smiley, wait."

"What can I do for you, Ma Mountain Goat, ma'am?"

"I just wanted to say. You've a home with us in Nova Scotia, if you want one."

"You can be our new brother," squealed Flora, throwing her arms around him. "We'll give you a bath."

"Flora!" scolded Ma.

Smiley's face glowed but he didn't answer.

Dougal noticed that Smiley's eyes weren't looking at Mam, they were looking at the ocean over her shoulder. "Come and live with us," said Dougal. "We'll have a fine time, and I won't let Flora bug you."

Flora punched him on the arm.

Smiley grinned briefly and shifted awkwardly on his feet. "I can't."

"Why not?"

"Don't get me wrong. I'm happier than a seagull hovering over a herring shoal that you've asked me. No one's ever wanted me before. But see, I'm a sailor, and I'm good at being a sailor. Never knew my Da but I bet he was a sailor too. It's like the sea's in my bones."

"What about the storm?" asked Dougal.

"I've stormy bones. Going to captain my own ship one day."

"You will," said Mam. "I know it."

At a shout from the Bosun, Smiley raced off. Dougal watched him go and wished he knew what was in his own bones.

"What I said to Smiley goes for you too, Johnny," said Mam. "You have a home with us if you want one."

"What I said goes too," laughed Dougal. "I won't let Flora bug you."

Flora kicked Dougal in the shin this time.

Johnny's face brightened then fell. "I would dearly love to be part of your family. But why would you want to be lumbered with someone as useless as me? I can hardly stand up."

"Ma will make you better," said Maggie, holding Johnny's hand.

"Fresh air, rest, solid ground, and some food inside you will do most of the work," said Mam.

Dougal looked Johnny straight in the eye and just said, "Please."

Johnny nodded. "I'd love to be part of your family. I feel I already am."

Dougal whooped while Flora and Maggie tried to give Johnny Piper a hug.

"I can't breathe," said Johnny.

"Leave the poor lad be," said Mam, pulling them off him. "Welcome to the family, Johnny Piper."

"Thank you," he said, managing a smile.

"Now that's settled let's get back to the matter in hand." She opened the lid of the sea chest and a puff of heather and lavender scented the sea air.

"Mmmm, it smells like home." Flora plunged her head into the chest for a longer sniff.

"Come away from there," said Mam, tugging on Flora's dress. "Whatever next?" Once Flora was out of the way, Mam pulled out Da's plaid. "Dougal, this is what you will wear to pipe us into our new life."

Dougal stared at the folded length of material that had been passed down from his grandfather. "There's a lot of history woven into this plaid," said Mam, as she expertly draped the material around Dougal. She tied the rope belt around his waist. "Wearing it today as you pipe us ashore is another part of its story." Dougal stood taller and a sense of pride mingled with his nervousness.

"But you've still got some growing to do," said Mam, hoisting the plaid up higher so it didn't touch his boots. She pleated the bottom section then arranged the top in careful folds over his shoulders. Dougal wished she'd hurry. He wanted to get the bagpipes out and have a quick practice.

"Stop fidgeting," said Mam. "You're worse than Flora."

"Here's Da's war bonnet," said Maggie.

Mam combed Dougal's hair, which had grown to below his shoulders, then placed the hat at an angle on his head. Her eyes glistened as she stood back to look at him. Even Flora gasped.

"You look like Da."

Dougal didn't know who he looked like. He definitely didn't feel like himself.

"Now the pipes," said Johnny Piper.

Dougal opened the bundle and assembled the instrument. His hands trembled. *It's funny*, he thought, *how being scared comes in all sorts of shapes and sizes.* This sort of scared was different from storm scared, or coming to an unknown place scared but it still tied his insides in knots.

"Leave off the drones," said Johnny Piper.

"No," said Dougal. "If I'm going to play, it's got to be the whole instrument." He could see the longboat being lowered into the water.

The Captain marched over, his eyes instantly taking in the situation. Directing his comments at Dougal, he said, "You'll be on the first boat, young fellow. The plan is for you to stand on the rocks and play that infernal instrument as each boatload of settlers step ashore. Come, don't keep us waiting."

Dougal hesitated. His mouth had suddenly gone very dry.

"You're a piper," whispered Maggie.

"Really?" asked Dougal.

Maggie nodded.

"You and Flora have to come with me," Dougal declared. "I need a drummer and a dancer.'

Grabbing Maggie's hand, Flora called, "See you in Nova Scotia, Mam," and followed Dougal and the Captain through the colourful crowd of weary, smiling faces to the other side of the ship.

"This horrific voyage is over," Dougal heard one settler say. "Our new life is beginning."

"But my poor bairn and seventeen others will never see this new land," said a woman, her words breaking into sobs.

I'll never get used to wearing this plaid, thought Dougal. *There's so much of it*. With one arm full of material and the other full of bagpipes, he managed to get one leg up and over the gunwale. As he struggled with his other one, the Bosun caught him round the waist.

"Can't say I'm sorry to see the last of you," he muttered as he lifted Dougal over the side and plonked him down on the bench like a helpless old grannie. "But good luck to you and your family. I wish you well."

"Thanks," said Dougal, a bit surprised.

The Bosun then lifted Flora and Maggie into the boat and they wriggled into position on either side of him.

The landing party pushed off from the *Hector* and after a few dips of the oars, the longboat grounded with a scrunch on the narrow strip of beach.

Climbing out of the longboat was as awkward as getting in, but Dougal managed it by himself, even though the bottom edge of Da's plaid trailed in the water.

"Hello, Nova Scotia," sang Flora, dancing ahead of him. She fell over. "I'm not used to the ground being still," she said in a fit of giggles. Dougal staggered after her. Walking on land really did feel odd. Maggie stayed stock-still at the water's edge.

"Come on, Maggie, you'll soon get used to walking on land again," said Dougal.

Maggie didn't move.

Once off the pebbles, Dougal stopped and looked around. He couldn't begin to imagine what his life would be like in this strange land of thick, dark forests. The tree in front of him was as straight and tall as the *Hector*'s mast and its branches filled the whole sky, just like in Mam's herbal book. Back home...he must stop saying "back home." Home wasn't backwards, it was forward. That's what Mam had said all those weeks ago. Good or bad, there was no going back. Through the trees, Dougal could see a few poor-looking dwellings. He'd expected a harbour or some sort of community, but there was nothing here—and where were the supplies? Da had told them there would be a whole year's worth to get them started.

The Captain marched along the beach, complaining loudly as he inspected the area. It was obvious he thought there'd be more, too. "Stand on that flat rock and play as the settlers arrive," he instructed. "They'll need something to distract them." The Captain returned to the *Hector*, leaving orders with two crew members to remain and get ready for the disembarkment.

Dougal breathed in the sweet, sharp smell of the pines. "A drink, first," he said to his sisters, and padded as quickly as he could over the soft forest floor to a stream he'd seen sparkling through the woods. Flora was right behind him. Maggie remained a statue at the water's edge.

"Come on," called Flora.

Maggie violently shook her head. "It's so dark in there. Look at those monster trees. They could be enormous tree monsters! I'm not going in there."

"They're friendly trees, you'll like them when you get to know them," said Flora. "Come and get a drink. We'll give them a hug later." Flora pulled Maggie along to where Dougal was gulping down cool, fresh water. He burped loudly, hiccupped, then choked on a mouthful.

"Easy, young fella," said a sailor, banging him on the back. "Slow down. Your insides aren't used to all this." Eventually Dougal's coughing and spluttering subsided. As he dipped for another drink, out of the corner of his eye he saw a rabbit dart through trees. His slingshot was still in his pocket and so was the sharp flint he'd used to carve the daily notches. There'd be supper tonight.

For now, the longboat was returning with the first group of settlers, and Dougal had a job to do. He wiped his mouth, freed the plaid from its tangle round his ankles, and climbed into position on the rock. He heaved the heavy instrument into place with the bag under his arm and the drones across his chest. He positioned his finger and blew down the blow pipe to inflate the bag. With his fingers on the chanter, he gently squeezed the bag with his arm until the drones breathed. *So far, so good.* As the settlers waded ashore, Dougal started playing. The first chords sounded good, but then he played a wrong note, lost concentration, and the pipes gave a protesting wail.

Dougal stopped blowing. He couldn't do this. What was he thinking? He wasn't a piper. He'd only been playing a short while, and until a few weeks ago he hadn't even seen a set of bagpipes.

At that moment he saw Malcolm help Isobel ashore with their new baby. She waved in his direction. Janet was in the boat too, with her arm around Mam. Dougal couldn't help smiling when he saw that Old Hugh had the job of carrying Wee Mary. Johnny Piper was slumped at the back.

Dougal suddenly realized bad chords didn't matter. It was the freedom to play that was the important thing. He started again, and a stumbly version of the "*Hector's Rain Song*," full of wrong notes, whines, stops and starts, rang through the trees of his new homeland. Maggie drummed the ground with Mam's wooden spoon, never once taking her eyes off the trees. Flora held her hands above her head, pointed her toes, and danced.

Dougal noticed a movement in the forest. Turning slightly, he saw folk from the huts coming through the trees to meet them. *They must have heard the pipes. Bagpipes really are magic.* Then Dougal recognized someone else standing in the swaying shadows of the evergreens. The blowpipe fell from his mouth and the music faded away.

"Don't stop," said Flora.

Dougal collected himself, took a deep breath, and began again. He played with his heart because he knew somewhere, somehow, his Da was listening.

THE STORY OF THE *HECTOR*

I HAVE ALWAYS LOVED SHIPS AND SAILING, AND after writing a story about the *Bluenose*, my attention was drawn to Nova Scotia's other full-sized tall-ship replica—the *Hector*. I knew the immense effort and expense involved in building a vessel like this meant there had to be a very important story behind it. And of course there was.

The *Hector* was the ship that brought the first significant wave of Scottish settlers to Nova Scotia. As time went by, these settlers spread out across the country. Many families in Canada today can trace their ancestry to the *Hector*'s passengers.

The background to this immigration story starts with the aftermath and consequences of the infamous Battle of Culloden, which took place in Scotland in 1746. A complicated dispute about the succession to the British throne led to this battle. Simply put, when Queen Anne died childless in 1714, there was no direct heir to the throne. By law, the king or queen of Britain had to be Protestant. The throne was passed to George I of the German House of Hanover. This caused a lot of resentment, especially in Scotland.

The Prince of Wales, James Francis Edward Stuart, was Queen Anne's Catholic half-brother. In 1688 he had had his title removed and was living in exile in France because he'd converted to Catholicism. His supporters were called Jacobites (the name came from Jacobus, Latin for James). The Jacobites believed that the Stuarts had a stronger claim to the British throne than the House of Hanover.

Over the years, five separate attempts were made to reinstate the Stuarts to the British throne. James Stuart's son, Charles Stuart, popularly known as Bonnie Prince Charlie, led the last attempt to claim the throne. He snuck back into Scotland and pulled together a small army of mainly Highlanders. As Charles travelled south, support for him grew. But in 1746, the Battle of Culloden, which took place on a boggy moor outside Inverness, brought the last rebellion to an end.

The Jacobites were defeated by the British army in a fight that only lasted forty minutes. The Duke of Cumberland, later nicknamed 'Butcher Cumberland,' ordered his men to hunt down and murder or imprison the surviving Jacobite rebels. Their villages were burned, their crops destroyed, and livestock slaughtered. The army seized and sold off land owned by Jacobite supporters.

In order to stop any more attempts to overthrow the king, power was taken away from the Scottish chiefs, and laws were passed to destroy the ancient culture of the clans. Wearing tartans or Highland dress, carrying weapons, and playing the bagpipes were all banned.

Life in the rugged Scottish Highlands had been difficult before the Battle of Culloden, and thirty years after, life for many families was unbearable. Farms were being subdivided, and landlords were forced to charge tenant farmers a higher rent. As the industrial revolution gained momentum, landlords from the south began replacing Highland cattle with sheep to supply the woollen mills in Northern England. It was very difficult for poor farming families to scratch out a living from the land.

In 1773, the year my story starts, the winter had been harder than usual and the fishing was poor. One day a notice appeared, advertising free farmland and supplies for a year to any family willing to settle in Nova Scotia, in the Americas. Living free on their own farm was every Highland farmer's dream. At first, people were reluctant to sign on. It was an offer that seemed too good to be true. Witherspoon and Pagan, the owners of the land in Nova Scotia that needed settling, hired a local man, John Ross, to promote the idea. People were convinced, and bought tickets for the voyage on the *Hector*.

ACKNOWLEDGEMENTS

I would like to thank:

The Access Copyright Foundation. With my research grant money, I was able to spend two weeks in Pictou, Nova Scotia. The cottage I rented was at Brown's Point, the exact place where the *Hector* passengers came ashore. I was able to walk around the town imagining the area as it was back in 1773, go to the museum, look at accounts of the voyage in some really old books, and visit the full-sized replica of the *Hector* as many times as I wanted.

Tom Ryan, my super editor, who helped a picture book writer become a novelist and didn't complain too much about my punctuation.

My dear writer's group friends: Marcia, Peggy, Vivien, and Marlene. Without them, my stories would never become books.

My husband, Ray, for his endless love and support.

Whitney Moran and the wonderful Nimbus team.

ABOUT
JACQUELINE HALSEY

Colin Bury

JACQUELINE HALSEY LIVES IN Dartmouth, Nova Scotia. In her books, she retells historical events through the eyes of children. *Peggy's Letters* and *Explosion Newsie* were both on the CCBC–Best Books for Children and Teens lists. When not writing, she spends her time teaching English to newcomers and helping take care of McNabs Island, a place overflowing with history.

Visit jacquelinehalsey.com.

GLOSSARY

bairn: A baby or small child.

breeks: Trousers.

cannae: Cannot.

ceilidh: An impromptu party with participants creating their own music and entertainment.

clan: A group of related Highland families.

croft: A small rented plot of farmland plus a cottage, with use of an area of common land shared with the other crofters.

dysentery: A disease caused by bad water and overcrowded, unsanitary living conditions.

New World: A name for what we now call the American continent. The term was first used during the time of exploration and colonization of the Americas by the Europeans.

peat: A turf-like material made of decomposed organic matter. It occurs in acidic, boggy areas. Because of its high carbon content, it can be cut into blocks or slabs, dried, and used for fuel.

smallpox: A highly contagious disease. Symptoms include fever and an oozy rash. It can be transmitted from an infected person to another by droplets in the air.

tartan: A cloth woven out of wool, in patterns of coloured checks. Each clan would have its own design. The colours may have meaning and significance.

NAUTICAL TERMS

Bosun: The Bosun is the senior crewman on deck and issues orders to the deck crew. He is responsible for the rigging, anchors, cables, sails, storing supplies, and inspecting the hull.

bow: The front part of the hull of a ship.

bulkhead: A partition wall in a ship.

capstan: A cylinder-shaped winch with spokes that are pushed around in a circle. It is used for hauling ropes. For example: when pulling up heavy sails.

gangway: A narrow passage on a ship.

gunwale: The thick wooden top edge of a ship's hull.

halliard: A rope used to hoist a sail.

hull: The main body of the ship excluding masts and rigging.

jib sail: A triangular sail set in front of the mast.

longboat: An open boat, rowed by several oarsmen. It would be carried on-board sailing vessels for ship-to-shore trips and as a lifeboat. Its design made it stable in surf or steep waves.

mizzen mast: A sailing ship with three masts has a foremast, a main mast and a mizzen mast. The mizzen mast is the smaller mast at the back of the vessel.

oakum: A product made of fibres, like straw or old rope, covered in tar, and used to seal the gaps between the timbers of wooden sailing ships.

porthole: A small round window in the ship's hull.

ratline: A type of rope ladder to make climbing into the rigging easier.

scuppers: Narrow openings in the side walls of the ship just above deck level to allow rain, wave splashes, or other water to drain out.

stern: The back part of the ship.

yardarm: The sideways poles attached to the masts from which the square sails are hung.